UNEXPECTED TREASURE . . .

The girl stared at Mannering. "Do you really want to see those pictures?" she asked, as though she couldn't believe him.

"I do indeed."

"It's dark up there. You'll need a candle."

"I've a torch," Mannering said. "Will you come up?"

The girl shivered, and shook her head. "I won't be more than five minutes," said Mannering. He went up the stairs, his shoulders touching the walls on either side. He pushed the ladder into position before the closed hatch of the attic, climbed up, and raised the hatch cover, holding the ladder with one hand.

Then he saw the man waiting above the hatch. His hand was raised, holding a heavy stick. Mannering made a grab for the ladder with both hands, then felt the stick crack down on his fingers. The pain was agonizing, and he let go, falling back . . .

D1413368

The Baron And The Missing Old Masters

John Creasey
writing as Anthony Morton

PRESTIGE BOOKS • NEW YORK

THE BARON AND THE MISSING OLD MASTERS

PRESTIGE BOOKS INC. • 18 EAST 41ST STREET
NEW YORK, N.Y. 10017

CHAPTER ONE

LETTER FROM A DEAR OLD LADY

John Mannering opened the letter without thinking much about it, for he was preoccupied with another, typewritten one from Rio de Janeiro, which reported that archaeologists in the Upper Amazon area had unearthed an old city and that in the temples there were bejewelled idols of great splendor and incalculable worth. The writer, Senhor Hortelez, was anxious to know whether Mannering would visit the long-lost city and examine the jewels and the enticing variety of rare antiques and *objets d'art* so newly discovered, with a view to selling them at Quinns in London, or Quinns in Boston, or through any of the sale-rooms with which Mannering was so familiar.

It was a most attractive prospect.

"We could do with a change," he mused, and glanced at a self-portrait of his wife, Lorna, on the wall opposite his desk in this small office at the back of Quinns in Hart Row, Mayfair. "Couldn't we?" he asked the picture, as he absent-mindedly slit open the second letter.

The envelope, with a Salisbury postmark, was addressed in a faltering hand: *Baron Mannering, Esq., Quinns, London.*

His smile broadened, then faded somewhat, for the

7

writing was spidery and almost indecipherable. At the top was the address, *Archway Cottage, Nether Wylie, Salisbury, Wilts*. The letter ran:

Dear Baron Mannering,

I read about you a lot, as I've always admired brave heroes and honest men. Have discovered in the attic some old oil pictures of my late husband's, which might be valuable, or again, might not. I don't trust dealers, but would trust you. Can't promise travel expenses, but if pictures okay I would look after you. Please come soon as I am seventy-seven years of age.

Eliza Doze

Mannering's smile broadened once again, and as he came to the name, he chuckled with real enjoyment. Surely, he told himself, it couldn't be true. He put the letter aside and opened others, none of any great significance, and all to do with the art world which was both his business and his life. But every now and again his gaze stole towards the letter from Eliza Doze, and finally he opened the Automobile Association handbook and looked for Nether Wylie; it wasn't there. He pressed a bell beneath the surface of his bow-shaped Queen Anne desk, and after a few moments gray-haired, gentle-voiced, kind-faced Josh Larraby came in. Larraby was the manager of Quinns of London. He was a little less than average height, and looked very short against Mannering's six feet one.

"Josh," Mannering said, "doesn't young Willis live near Salisbury?"

"He does indeed, sir."

"Ask him if he knows of a place named Nether Wylie, and if he does, send him in."

"Right. You know that Mrs. Besborough is coming at ten o'clock, don't you?" Larraby urged.

"I remember." Mannering looked at the invitation

8

from Rio de Janeiro again. Enticing was the word for it. There was no great urgency, however. The suggested date was a week ahead, giving him time enough to go to Nether Wylie for a day or two.

There was a tap at the door.

"Come in," Mannering called.

The young man who came in, rather diffidently, was tall and willowy and black-haired, good-looking in a long-faced, almost saturnine way. He had very large brown eyes, upsweeping lashes and clearly defined eyebrows. And he dressed exquisitely. He had been at Quinns for nearly a year, being one of a stream of young men who came to train for a profession which was both cultural and commercial, had a special *panache* and required a great deal of specialized knowledge and a shrewd power of assessment. This one was Beverley Willis, son of Lord Amplesham, and many had made the grave mistake of believing that his dandyism spelt effeminacy.

"Good morning, sir."

"Good morning, Willis. Do you know a village called Nether Wylie?"

"I know it well," answered Willis. "A nice little trout stream runs through it, linking up with the Wiltshire Avon. Colonel Cunliffe lives at Nether Manor; the Cunliffes have been there for centuries." He broke off, as if afraid that his enthusiasm was running away with him.

"You don't know an Eliza Doze, do you?"

"Eliza, Eliza?" Willis frowned, delicately. "No, sir, I don't think I know an Eliza; though Doze does have a slightly feudal ring in my mind as being associated with the Cunliffes. But the name is fairly common in Wiltshire."

"So Eliza Doze is probably a real name?"

"No reason at all why it shouldn't be," said Willis. "The two names seem to fit very snugly together."

"Possibly," said Mannering drily, "but I'm not looking

9

for a study in euphony. Are the Dozes you know, or have heard of, reliable families?"

"Very reliable indeed," Willis assured him. "The only black sheep I remember was Ezekiel Doze. Good heavens, sir! I *do* know an Eliza, she used to be nanny to Colonel Cunliffe's daughters before she married Ezekiel. He was a second-hand dealer, the kind that used to be called a rag-and-bone man, and spent most of what little he earned on drink. But he must have been dead for ten years or more; I can only just remember him."

Willis's interest showed in his eyes but he refrained from voicing it.

"And Eliza wants me to go down and look at some oil pictures," Mannering said solemnly.

"Some oil—*oh*," Willis smiled, almost pained. "*Her* phraseology, sir?"

"Yes."

"Aren't there enough art dealers or antique dealers in Salisbury?" Willis asked. "The city's full of them, and very good ones, too. At least two are excellent judges of paintings."

"Eliza Doze doesn't trust them."

"Oh," said Willis, and wrinkled his long nose. "Probably a bit clannish as a family, and I seem to remember some kind of sensation." He contemplated Mannering for some time, before going on: "I could find out more, without any trouble. I know the Cunliffes quite well."

"Talk to them on the telephone, will you?"

"As a matter of fact, sir, one of the daughters lives in town. I might be able to find out something during lunch."

"See if she's free," Mannering said, and was fully aware of the satisfaction which appeared in Willis's eyes.

As he spoke, the telephone rang. Mannering lifted the receiver.

"Mrs. Besborough is here, sir," Larraby informed him.

"Thanks, Josh—all right, Willis, let me know what you can."

"If she isn't free this morning I'll have a shot this evening," Willis promised.

He opened the door, stepping aside for Mannering to enter the long, narrow shop to welcome Mrs. Besborough, who was standing by Larraby. The contrast between them was quite remarkable, Larraby being almost part of the background of oak paneling and beautiful paintings, of discreetly lit show-cases containing jewellery and *bibelots* of great antiquity and interest, while Mrs. Besborough, very tall, very angular, was the last word in modernity of dress and manner. A woman of sixty, she had quite beautiful legs and a frank and uninhibited desire to show them. She was a South African with a great deal of money and had come to buy for a museum in a town in the Orange Free State. Mannering had learned already that she was an excellent business woman, knew what she wanted to buy, and would not waste his time.

They shook hands.

"Mr. Mannering, I've decided *not* to take the Georgian silver, but I *am* interested in the mediaeval armor and the jewelled swords and lances. I feel that there will be a great deal of interest shown in them in South Africa. And I seem to remember a twelfth-century set of Black Forest hunting spears that would be of general interest, too . . ."

Mannering spent most of the morning with her, then lunched off a sandwich and beer while he dictated letters. There were only two he did not answer—those from Eliza Doze and Senhor Hortelez; he could not make up his mind about either, and wanted to talk to Lorna about the South American possibility. If she were free from painting commissions and would like to come, they could mix business with pleasure. Immediately after lunch he

11

went to Christie's for a preview; there were some inter-esting Dutch portraits, but nothing he wanted for him-self. A Chinese oil lamp of the Fourth Ming Dynasty caught his eye. He made a mental note of the price he would give for it; possibly he would send someone to bid. He was so preoccupied that he forgot Eliza Doze and was walking into the street when he heard his name called in a foreign accent.

"Mr. Mannairing, pliz—Mr. Mannairing!" He turned, to see a small, dark-haired man half in, half out of a taxi— Jules Corot, a French antique dealer with whom he did a lot of business.

". . . I telephoned your gallery but you were not there, and I must fly back to Paris tonight, I come only for the day. Did you have the letter from Hortelez this morning?"

"Yes," answered Mannering.

"*Bien!* He tells me you hear from him. I have a client very interested indeed, he will spend a million francs at least if the jewels are genuine, but alas I cannot go to South America next week. Can you go, pliz?"

"I'm thinking of it," Mannering temporized.

Corot's eyes lit up.

"Good! I am very glad if you will, I would rather trust your judgment of the discovery. There is talk, you know, of a clever fake. These cities are so soon buried under the jungle, it is possible a patch was cleared and a false temple and idols put there a few years ago, then al-lowed to be grown over. You understand me?"

"Very well," said Mannering.

"Will you talk by telephone if you are going?"

"Yes, of course. By the end of the week."

"*Bien!* Mr. Mannairing, forgive pliz, I have a client I meet at Christie's. He is interested in some tapestries said to be Norman—did you see them?"

"I only noticed them in passing," Mannering said.

Corot pouted. "What you only notice in passing is often not worth stopping to look at. But I must go!" He gripped Mannering's hand, and hurried into the entrance to the sale-rooms and up the stairs.

Mannering walked briskly back to Quinns. Not until he reached the shop did he think again of Eliza Doze, reminded by the sight of Beverley Willis at the door. Pausing to study a single jewelled headpiece, said to have belonged to the Tsarina, he nodded approval of the way Larraby had placed it, and went inside. Three customers were in the shop, which had the curiously subdued atmosphere of a museum rather than a place of business.

"How did you get on at lunch?" Mannering asked Willis.

"Oh, splendidly, thanks." Obviously the young man had lunched well and the stars were still in his eyes. "Oh, and I *was* right about the sensation. It was some time ago, of course, but these things never seem to die, and only gather more lustre with the years and the telling. It appears old Ezekiel Doze sold a painting for a few shillings to a Salisbury dealer and it resold at Christie's for five thousand. Doze drank himself silly on what little the dealer had given him—and refused to go near a dealer again."

Mannering saw one of the customers glance up, as if with sudden interest.

He was a middle-aged, graying man with small, very bright eyes, and had been talking to one of the younger assistants about a Queen Anne cabinet. Mannering went along to his office, giving the man only a passing thought.

On top of his desk was the letter from Eliza Doze. He read it again—and quite suddenly he decided: I'll go down and see her. It was now nearly three o'clock and there was no time to drive to Nether Wylie and back before night—but if he caught an early train the next

13

morning he could hire a car in Salisbury and go round and see the local antique shops; he hadn't been to the cathedral city for a long time.

His telephone bell rang.

"Mannering . . . Oh, hallo, darling! . . . Believe it or not, I've been thinking about you."

"And I've been thinking about you," his wife told him. She had a deep voice for a woman, and now, as so often, it held a note of laughter. "I ran into Jules Corot and he told me about Rio de Janeiro. If you go without me——"

Mannering's heart leapt.

"Can you come?"

"Yes—bless you, darling!"

"Wonderful," said Mannering. "We'll fly next Tuesday, there's a plane which gets us to Rio just in time. Can you be ready?"

"I will be, but I'll have to work like mad," Lorna said. "I've promised Mrs. Besborough her portrait by Monday, and this will be an added incentive. Have you noticed what a strangely hawk-like face she has?"

"Eagle," Mannering hazarded.

"Both predatory birds," said Lorna, "so take care. I may work late tonight; don't worry if I sleep up in the studio."

She rang off.

Mannering put down the receiver, smiling, faintly nostalgic. Not very long ago his marriage had seemed in grave danger of breaking, but both had realized this in time; now each knew a fresh sense of contentment with and enjoyment of each other.

There was a tap at the door; it was the assistant who had been with the bright-eyed man.

"What is it?" asked Mannering, absently.

"Mr. Jenkins would very much like a word with you, sir. He says he has a matter he would like to discuss in confidence."

"Do you know Mr. Jenkins?" asked Mannering.

14

"He has just taken over The Kettle in Salisbury," the other answered. "We have dealt with them in the past."

"From Salisbury," Mannering echoed, under his breath. "The long arm of coincidence? I wonder." Louder, he went on: "Yes, of course. Show Mr. Jenkins in."

CHAPTER TWO

THE MAN FROM THE KETTLE

Mr. Jenkins had soft, cool hands and soft, cool-looking cheeks and soft, down-like hair which grew in side-whiskers and moustache as if in a persistent attempt to assert manliness. He was hesitant in manner, and sat on the edge of the big armchair fashioned for a much larger man. He took one timid glance about the office and then his gaze lingered on the portrait above Mannering's head. As Mannering spoke, to put him at his ease, he started, shooting a look at Mannering and then another at the portrait, which was of a man in the hat, ringlet curls and furbelows of a cavalier. The heads were as like as two peas, strong, handsome and dark-haired, the slightly arched eyebrows identical.

"How can I help you, Mr. Jenkins?" Mannering asked.

"Why that—why, it's the spitting image of *you*," declared Jenkins, on a rising note of excitement. "I'm sorry if I appear rude, but you must admit the likeness is a bit startling. What did you say, sir?"

Mannering smiled. "It *is* me," he announced.

"Eh?" Jenkins's gaze darted up and down, up and down.

"It is me—the portrait is of me."

Jenkins's mouth opened wide.

"You mean——" He was baffled.

"I'm in fancy dress," explained Mannering. "My wife thought it a great joke."

"Wife?" echoed Jenkins, as if the introduction of this new element was too much for him. His gaze swiveled round again and he caught sight of the portrait of Lorna.

It was time to get the situation completely under control, Mannering decided. He sat upright and his voice deepened.

"My wife is a portrait painter and she painted me as a cavalier. The portrait you're looking at now is a self-portrait of my wife. Now! How can I help you, Mr. Jenkins?"

Jenkins turned back, gulped, and said: "It's very kind of you to see me, I'm sure."

"If it's a personal matter——" Mannering began, belatedly wondering if this man was a particularly clever confidence trickster, or even a beggar who found that this ingenuous manner paid dividends.

"Oh, no, Mr. Mannering, it's business. You see, I—I'm in the trade. I'm a runner, so to speak—you know what a runner is, sir, don't you?"

"You mean you go from gallery to gallery offering paintings for sale, or take pictures to the framers and restorers."

Jenkins's expression cleared.

"That's it, sir, right on the nose! I don't work in London, mind you, only in the provinces, south-west mostly, that's how I came to take over The Kettle. You know The Kettle, in Salisbury, don't you?"

"Slightly," Mannering said.

"It's a very nice shop, a very nice shop indeed, but the gentleman who had it before me wasn't very knowledgeable about the trade, sir, if you know what I mean. He had favorites, and it's never any good to hold on to pieces just because you like them, is it? The business went down and down, as a matter of fact, and I bought it, wanting a place of my own, as you might say."

"You were tired of acting as a runner," said Mannering, patiently.

"That's it, sir—right on the nose. I'd just met Miss Right, too, and she had a little bit saved so we took over The Kettle. You should see it now, sir—a shop to be proud of, even though I say it myself."

"I'm sure it is," murmured Mannering.

"And I know the district well, know all the big houses and all the little ones, sir—I know the business though I do say it myself. But to cut a long story short, sir, I came across some real beauties last week, absolute beauties— but I'm not sure what they're worth. What I was wondering, sir, was whether a gentleman like you would come and have a look at them?"

"In Salisbury?" asked Mannering, unbelieving.

"I'd pay your expenses, sir, it wouldn't cost you anything except a bit of time and it *would* be in the way of business. I've also picked up some fifteenth-century pewter—I know my pewter, Mr. Mannering, don't make any mistake about that. You buy pewter, don't you?"

"Sometimes," said Mannering. "Are these paintings in your shop?"

"Oh, no, they belong to an old crone—an old lady in a village outside Salisbury, sir. As a matter of fact, it's a grand-daughter of the old lady who knows my wife Dora, and Dora put me on to these paintings so I went and had a look. She doesn't live far out—a village called Nether Wylie; I don't know whether you've heard of it?"

Mannering did not speak.

"And I'd run you out there in my car," offered Mr. Jenkins. "The old lady doesn't trust dealers, and she wouldn't take my offer, so before I make a bigger one I want to be sure I'm on the right track."

18

"Yes," said Mannering drily, "I'm sure you do. My fee for a valuation is fairly high, Mr. Jenkins."

"Oh, I don't want a valuation," Jenkins almost squealed. "My idea was, that if you think they're worth a gamble, we would go into it together. There's no doubt about it, Mr. Mannering; if a man like me is on to a good thing the trade beats him down, but a man with your reputation and your knowledge of the market—you'd get twice, *three* times the amount I would. It isn't far, Mr. Mannering, and I think these are worth a look, really I do."

"Can you bring one to show me?" asked Mannering.

"I suppose I could try," said Jenkins dubiously, "but she won't part with them easy, I know that. Wouldn't you consider coming down and taking a look yourself, Mr. Mannering?"

Mannering said musingly: "I may be near Salisbury this week."

Jenkins's eyes lit up.

"Then that's wonderful, sir! I can arrange for you to see them any time on Sunday morning, between half-past ten and half-past twelve, the old bit—the old lady goes to church then and the grand-daughter would let us in. Just between you and me," went on Jenkins, leaning forward intently, "we could get the lot for a hundred pounds and if I'm right we'd make a fortune. I *think* one of them's a Vermeer. A rare bargain," he added, as if the word turned to nectar on his lips.

At first Mannering had felt sorry for Mr. Jenkins, but gradually he had grown to dislike him, and now his dislike was acute indeed. Mr. Jenkins was quite prepared to buy the paintings for a song and make a fortune out of them, leaving Eliza Doze—for Eliza Doze it must be, reflected Mannering—with all her old distrust of dealers strengthened to bitterness. Yet Mannering did not show what he felt. Had he any doubt before, this would have decided him to go to Salisbury. If the paintings were by

19

a freak of chance genuine, this man was the last one, in his opinion, worthy of getting his hands on them. Even if they were good copies they would be comparatively valuable.

"Where can I get in touch with you?" he asked.

"Oh, at The Kettle, sir, at The Kettle. There's living accommodation over the shop. Real old place it is, sixteenth century. I will say the previous owner made a real good job of it when he took it over. Put in a bathroom and all the mod cons—it couldn't be more up to date. Dora thinks it's lovely. I'll see you down there, then."

"Yes," said Mannering.

Mr. Jenkins held out a moist hand.

"That's splendid, Mr. Mannering, couldn't suit me better. I've a few old pals in London I ought to see, and Dora's looking after the shop. Not that she knows the trade at all but everything's marked clearly. Fair dealing's my motto, Mr. Mannering. So I'll just pop along to find out what my pals are looking for; never know when I mightn't come across the very thing."

Mannering ushered him out of the office, then out of the front door. He went off, obviously jubilant. Mannering turned, to see Larraby snapping the fastening of a small display case filled with Napoleonic miniatures—Bonaparte on horseback, on foot, sitting, drinking, eating, even sleeping, the colors having strangely retained their depth throughout the years.

"Excuse me, sir."

"Yes, Josh?"

"Did you recognize that visitor?"

"Jenkins?" asked Mannering.

"Oliver *Fenks* is the name," said Larraby. "Or it used to be. Your own kindness to me after *I* came out of prison will always be an object lesson in human charity, sir, and I wouldn't hold a prison sentence against any man. But Oliver Fenks is notorious."

Mannering frowned. "In what particular way?" he asked.

"For dealing in forged and stolen paintings, sir. He served his sentence for conspiracy with two other men to break into a gallery and steal a collection of Flemish masters. And he betrayed his accomplices, sir, in the hope of getting a lighter sentence."

"And did he?"

"If my memory serves me he was sentenced to five years in prison and if he behaved himself he no doubt came out after three and a half," Larraby answered. "I really don't want to victimize the man for his past, but he looked so pleased with himself when he left that——" Larraby broke off.

"You were afraid he'd fooled me," Mannering said drily.

"I'm very glad that he didn't," Larraby said.

"I suppose I can't really be sure what he's after. Come into the office, Josh." Mannering told Larraby exactly what had passed between him and the runner, and while Larraby was reading Eliza Doze's letter, looked up the Railway ABC.

As Larraby glanced up, Mannering closed the book.

"It is very peculiar indeed," Larraby remarked. "What do you think of it, sir?"

"Either Jenkins *alias* Fenks thinks he's on to a good thing," Mannering said, "or Eliza Doze has told this grand-daughter of hers that she's approached me, and Jenkins, having heard of this, has come to stake a claim. He's going to be in London overnight at least, and there's a train to Salisbury at five o'clock this afternoon. I'll need a taxi while I'm there—ring through and reserve one for me, will you?"

"I will, sir!" Larraby was delighted.

"And put off any appointments for tomorrow," Mannering ordered. "I'll telephone you in the morning." He

21

glanced at his watch. "I've an hour yet. Tell Audrey to get the longer letters done first."

Picking up an overnight case which he always kept at the shop, he unpacked it, pressed a spot at one side, then pulled up a false panel. Beneath this was a set of tools, some thin but very strong nylon rope, and a small gas pistol with its supply of tear-gas pellets. He checked these contents and made sure the pistol was loaded, then put it back in the case. When the false panel was again in position, he replaced the spare shirts, ties, collars, handkerchiefs, a light-weight dressing-gown, slippers, shaving gear and a paperback copy of Byron's poems; everything in fact designed to give pleasure and comfort if he were away from home for a night or two.

Exactly an hour later he was sitting in a corner seat of a crowded train. And at five minutes to seven he was standing on the platform of Salisbury station.

"Where will I find a taxi which should be waiting for me?" he asked a porter.

"Just outside, sir, and round to the right." The porter waved towards the station entrance.

The taxi was a Ford, the driver a youthful-looking but nearly bald man with a pleasant manner and a rather husky voice. Mannering got in at the back and, out of habit, looked round to make sure that no one followed him; except for two taxis which turned off near the station yard, no one did.

"First stop Nether Wylie, sir, isn't it?" the driver asked.

"Please," Mannering said.

"Best go Wilton way from here," advised the driver. "Any particular house, sir?"

"I'm looking for somewhere to do some fishing later in the month," Mannering replied. "I'm told this is a good area."

"Very good, sir, you won't find a better in this part of the world for trout. Get a few salmon, too. But you won't find anywhere to stay overnight at Nether Wylie, it's only a few cottages, and the Manor, the church and a pub. There's no *hotel*, sir."

"I'll look round when I'm there," said Mannering.

The journey took longer than he had expected, winding through country lanes already showing the first signs of autumn, and alongside a narrow stream rippling under the bowed branches of bankside trees. Here and there were cottages, a village, a rose-colored wall with eaves over it; everywhere the quiet of evening was settling. Only now and again did they pass a car, only once a man on a bicycle. At last, a grey stone building with a thatched roof loomed up, and a swinging inn sign bearing the words *Nether Inn*. The windows, Mannering noticed, were leaded and the doorway narrow. Beyond a small car park were two pairs of cottages, and a by-road flanked by beech trees through which more roofs and chimneys could be seen. Right at the end of the village, standing on its own, was a cottage with a slate roof, plain, even ugly, with an overgrown yew hedge about it and a tangle of ramblers which had obviously not been pruned for some years.

At the door was a policeman, talking to a girl who appeared to be both pretty and agitated. As the taxi stopped, Mannering heard her say:

"But there's nothing here worth stealing, that's the puzzling thing, nothing at all." After a pause, she added: "She will be all right, won't she? They'll look after her at the hospital, won't they?"

Judging from the tone of her voice she was near despair.

Mannering thought: Nothing to *steal!* And then he pictured the shaky handwriting of the old woman's written plea. He had lost no time—but even so he might have arrived too late.

CHAPTER THREE

THE ATTIC

The policeman, young and sturdy, and the girl, who lost some of her prettiness as Mannering drew nearer along the path leading to the cottage, both turned to stare at him.

"Good evening, sir," said the policeman.

"Good evening. Is Mrs. Eliza Doze at home?" Mannering asked.

"I'm afraid not, sir. She's met with an accident."

"*Accident!*" cried the girl. "She was attacked, brutally attacked!"

"May I ask what your business is, sir?" the policeman asked.

"Mrs. Doze asked me to come and see her," Mannering answered. "My name is——"

"Baron!" exclaimed the girl, the name bursting out of her. "You've come already!" She pushed the policeman aside, and turned an agitated face to Mannering. "Oh, if only you'd come an hour ago!"

"Excuse me, sir," said the policeman doggedly, "but I need to get the situation clear for my report. Mrs. Doze *asked* you to come and see her?"

"Yes, she——"

"It's Baron Mannering!" exclaimed the girl.

"Just Mr. Mannering," Mannering corrected, "but sometimes I've been called the Baron. Mrs. Doze told me she had come across some old pictures in her attic, and wanted me to have a look at them."

"They weren't any good," the girl declared, "I told her they were a lot of old rubbish, but it was never any use talking to Granny. She—oh, I don't know what to do. I'm so worried."

"Are you planning to stay, sir?" inquired the policeman.

"As I'm here I'd like to look at the pictures—but can I help Mrs. Doze?"

"No, sir, she's in the Infirmary, and as well as can be expected. I'll go and make my report if you'll wait with Miss Doze until I'm back."

"I simply can't stay by myself tonight!" the girl said, with a catch in her breath.

"Don't you worry, lass, we'll fix something," the policeman assured her. He turned and swung a leg over his bicycle, which had been leaning against the inside of the overgrown hedge. The girl watched him pedal off, saw him raise a hand in greeting to the taxi driver, and then turned to Mannering. She clutched his arm.

"You won't go away, will you?"

"Certainly not until you're looked after," Mannering assured her. "May I see the paintings?"

"Well, yes, if you don't mind climbing into the attic." She led the way into a small square parlour, sparsely furnished, but much better kept than the outside of the cottage. A narrow staircase led upwards, and from a landing at the top rose a ladder which stood vertically against the wall. "I don't know how Granny ever got up there."

"What exactly happened to your grandmother?" Mannering asked.

"Well, I don't rightly know, sir. She hasn't been very

25

well lately, and my mum having gone away for a few days, I was staying with Gran. I'd been in to Salisbury on the bus and as I was walking along the lane I heard a scream. So I came running. I could hardly believe my eyes! There was a man in the doorway, and Granny on the floor with blood all over her head."

"What happened to the man?"

"He must have run away," the girl answered. "I screamed and screamed, and two telephone men happened to be passing. If it hadn't been for them I don't know what would have happened. One of them phoned for the ambulance and the police and the other one came in with me, I felt so scared."

"I should think so," Mannering said. "Did the man have anything with him?"

"Nothing big, if that's what you mean. It couldn't be those pictures that are worth stealing, could it?"

"It's obviously possible," said Mannering.

"Oh, they can't be! I—I told Granny they weren't worth ten bob apiece. I—I've a friend in Salisbury, you see, and her husband said he'd buy them on spec; he offered twenty-five pounds for the lot. Imagine, twenty-five pounds!" She caught her breath. "But supposing they *are* valuable? You must think they are, or you wouldn't have come!"

"I happened to be near," lied Mannering soothingly, "and your grandmother wrote such a charming letter."

The girl paused at the foot of the staircase. "And you really want to see them?" she asked.

"I do indeed."

"It's dark up there. You'd need a candle."

"I've a torch," Mannering said. "Will you come up?"

The girl shivered, with an exaggerated shake of her head.

"Then go and talk to the taxi driver," Mannering advised. "I won't be more than five minutes."

He waited for the girl to start walking along the path, then went up the stairs, his shoulders touching the walls on either side. There was a fusty smell as he neared the landing. Above it was a closed hatch into the attic. Pushing the ladder into position, Mannering climbed halfway up, then raised the hatch cover, which fell back with the groaning of rusty hinges. He went up two more rungs, marveling that any old person could make such a climb.

Then he saw the eyes.

There, in the attic, was a man, glaring down at him, a man with his hand raised and a heavy stick in it.

Mannering, poised on the ladder, one hand on the side of the hatch, felt his heart turn over. He made a desperate effort to grab the ladder with both hands, then felt the stick crack down on his fingers. The pain was agonizing. He let go. The drop was only a few feet but he landed awkwardly, banging his head so heavily on the wall that he felt everything go hazy and dark. As he staggered, clinging desperately to consciousness, he saw something fall, a loose roll, awkward in shape. Another and another followed and he realised that they were canvases.

The shock of the realization partially brought him round.

Four more canvases fell before he saw first the feet, then the legs of the man in the attic. One moment he seemed to be above Mannering's head, the next he landed heavily on the floor, keeping his balance without any sign of fear.

Mannering crouched low as the other picked up the canvases and tried to roll them inside one another. The last one foiled him in its stiffness and he tossed it impatiently down the stairs, and started after it.

Mannering threw himself forward, arms outstretched, and grabbed his assailant by the leg, just below the knee. The man twisted round in a desperate effort to save himself from falling, but lost his footing and went tumbling down the stairs, the canvases after him as the roll unfurled. Mannering, still dazed and in pain, stood up slowly and leaned against the wall. The man lay still. Was it Mannering's imagination, or was his head bent at an awkward angle—as if the neck were broken?

Drawing in a dozen long, deep breaths, Mannering began to go down the stairs, still leaning against the wall as he did so. He stepped over the other, carefully, but kicked one of the canvases; it gave a crunching sound. If it were really old, such treatment was sacrilege. Gradually, painfully, he maneuvered himself into a position in which he could feel his assailant's pulse.

At first, he felt no beating.

He stared into the pale, round turnip of a face, the bulging eyes protuberant even beneath the lids: those glaring eyes which had been so frightening. There was slight movement of the full lips—ah! The pulse *was* beating. Carefully, Mannering felt all over the man's body; no bones seemed to be broken. He eased him down the last few stairs, carried him into the parlor and stretched him out on an old saddleback sofa which had its back to the window.

The man seemed dead to the world, but Mannering hesitated, then went into the kitchen. In a drawer he found a tangled ball of string, and with this he bound the man's hands and ankles; then he ran through his pockets. They contained only a wallet with a few pounds in it, a driving licence in the name of Harry Anstiss, with an address in Shepherd's Bush, W.12, some stamps and a *Drivers' Club* credit card also in the name of Anstiss and with the same address.

Mannering stood upright.

Through the diamond-shaped panes of the window he saw the girl and the taxi driver animatedly talking. He heard her laugh, happy in her chance of relating the tale of drama yet again. Going into the lobby at the foot of the stairs, he picked up the canvases.

There were seven in all. He straightened them out carefully and took them to the kitchen, which faced north; the evening light was better here than from any other point of the compass, but the kitchen window was too small to allow much in. Mannering opened the door and stepped outside with three of the paintings under his arm.

He began to feel the quickening of his heartbeat, and a tension he had not known for some time. If these pictures were genuine discoveries he was holding something priceless in his hands—not priceless simply in terms of money, but in terms of art.

If only the light were better!

He spread one picture out over a covered water-butt. The picture was old-looking, with subdued colors and in the Dutch school of the seventeenth century. This was a family scene; a mother and a child, a man and two younger men in the background, light streaming through a window of a cottage in the way which Vermeer had mastered so completely.

It *could* be!

Mannering felt a choking kind of excitement at the very possibility, then placed another canvas over the first. This was an outdoor scene, with many tiny figures conveying a controlled sense of movement along a village street. *Breughel?* It was just possible, but he did not think he could form a really sound opinion until morning—or at least until he could examine the canvas under the right kind of intensive light. It was no use looking at the third, the background of which was darker.

He gathered up the pictures, and as he did so, saw a movement out of the corner of his eye. He turned, quickly. A girl was crossing the end of the garden, obviously anxious not to be seen, for as he turned she

29

sprang forward and disappeared behind a thick hedge. Mannering hesitated for a moment, then, with a vision of the girl's slim figure, dark hair and almost scared face still in his mind's eye, he took the pictures back into the kitchen, looking about for a way of keeping them protectively packed. Finding some old newspapers, he placed several sheets between each painting, then tied them in a package with several lengths of string. By the time he had finished it was getting dark, and it did not surprise him to see the taxi driver and the girl approaching along the path.

What would they say when they saw the bound figure on the sofa?

The man's eyes were now wide open, and Mannering remembered acutely the way they had glared down at him from the attic.

"You—you're Mannering," the prisoner said.

"Yes," Mannering replied, "and you're Anstiss."

The man nodded. "Give me the pictures," he mumbled hoarsely, "give me the pictures and let me go, and there's a thousand quid in it for you."

"I'll manage without the thousand," Mannering said, drily.

"Let me—let me get out of here," Anstiss pleaded. There was something peculiarly agitated in his manner, as if he were listening for something. "Why don't you——?"

There was a muffled explosion above their heads. Anstiss started violently.

"Get me out of here. *Get me out!*" Something near panic was in his voice and his expression as he began to struggle against his bonds. "Cut me loose!" he cried. "If you don't——"

There was a second, lesser explosion, and as it died away the taxi driver shouted:

"Look there!"

Mannering glanced out of the window and saw both man and girl staring towards the roof of the cottage. Almost at that instant the taxi driver bellowed:

"You in there, get out! The place is on fire!"

"Let me go!" screeched the man on the sofa.

Mannering swung round towards the door as the taxi driver appeared. He saw Mannering and his prisoner, and stopped short, his mouth open.

"Take these," Mannering said calmly. He thrust the package into the taxi driver's arms, spun round again and picked Anstiss up, then strode towards the door. He could hear hissing and crackling, he even imagined he could feel the heat. The front door was still open, the driver a few yards along the path.

Mannering ran.

As he reached the roadway he turned again and saw the whole of the roof on fire, flames shooting vertically into the air; and now he could indeed feel the heat, fiercely, furiously beating at him. He moved towards the taxi, and bundled Anstiss into it. Straightening up, he saw people hurrying from the main street of the village, the policeman on his bicycle at their head.

One thing was certain; no ordinary domestic fire could have gathered force at such speed. This one had obviously started with those muffled explosions; petrol, or something similarly combustible, had caught alight instantaneously.

Another thing was equally certain; anything left in that attic, whether priceless or not, had gone forever.

Were the paintings which the man Anstiss had brought away of value?

As the question passed through Mannering's mind, he heard the clip-clop of hoofbeats, and once again he saw the girl who had been in the back garden of the cottage. The horse was cantering and she sat beautifully, with the natural ease of a rider who had been used to the saddle

31

since childhood. The reflection of the flames tinted her dark hair a Titian red, and there was a blaze of fire in her eyes.

She glanced into the taxi—and fear was added to the fire.

CHAPTER FOUR

MISS JOANNA

The girl reined in her horse. As she sprang from the saddle Mannering saw her lips move. Then, leading the horse, she drew nearer to the little bunch of people gathered at the gate.

"Good evening, Miss Joanna," the policeman called, touching his helmet, "I've just been talking to the Colonel."

"Have you, Cope?" The girl's voice was quite calm and her manner normal enough. "What about?"

"About Betsy here," the constable answered. "Her grandmother's been hurt and she doesn't want to stay ——" He broke off, glancing up at the ravening tongues of fire, and added rather helplessly: "Not that she could, anyway."

"You must come to the house, Betsy," Joanna said promptly.

"That's what the Colonel said," the policeman reported.

"Thank you, Miss, thank you ever so much." The girl was almost in tears. "What a thing to happen!" she gasped. "All Granny's furniture gone—everything."

"We'll see that she's looked after," Joanna promised,

33

and turned to Mannering. "Are you Mr. Mannering? Beverly Willis's employer?" She still spoke calmly.

"Yes," said Mannering.

"I wonder if you can spare a moment."

"Of course."

"The fire brigade should be along any minute," said the policeman. "You'll look after Betsy, then, Miss Joanna?"

"Yes, Cope, don't worry about her."

Had the constable glanced into the taxi he must have seen the prisoner, but his head was turned and his gaze uplifted towards the fire.

"Mr. Mannering," Joanna said in a very low-pitched but firm voice, "will you please let this man go?"

Mannering was startled into exclaiming: "*What?*"

"It's extremely important—please, Mr. Mannering, I beg you not to take him to the police."

Constable Cope was talking to the crowd and pointing towards the flying sparks. The more prudent of them turned and moved away. In a few seconds someone was bound to notice that the man in the taxi was tied; questions would be asked, and the ensuing publicity would make it impossible for Mannering to do what the girl wished. He had to make a snap decision.

"Can you guarantee that he won't run away?" he asked tersely.

"No." Joanna answered. "I can only promise an explanation." She stretched her hands towards him until they almost touched his, but did not speak again.

For good or ill Mannering made the decision.

Taking a penknife from his pocket he leaned inside the car and cut the string at the man's wrists and ankles. Anstiss struggled to a sitting position, then slithered feet first out on to the road.

"Okay," he muttered. "I'll keep mum."

He turned and walked boldly towards the policeman and the thickening crowd. Three cars and some motor-

cyclists stopped, and the man slipped unobtrusively between them.

Joanna said huskily: "Thank you—thank you very
much."

"I hope you can convince me that I've done the right
thing," Mannering said drily.

"I—I think I can. Are you staying in Salisbury
tonight?"

"I haven't a hotel yet, but——"

"Then please stay with us! My father would be delighted, and——" She broke off, finishing simply: "I will
have a chance to talk to you."

"If you're sure it's all right."

"Of course it is," said Joanna. "If you'll take Betsy in
the taxi she can show you the way, and the housekeeper
will look after her. I'll ride across country and tell Daddy
you're coming." Climbing quickly into the saddle, she
turned the horse and waved a casual goodbye.

There was nothing left for Mannering to do, for more
than enough villagers and passers-by were at hand to
cope with any danger from flying sparks, and he could
already hear the clanging bell of the approaching fire-
engine. Motioning to the taxi driver, who still held the
package of canvases, he beckoned to Betsy.

The driver glanced at the empty back seat. "Wasn't
there a man——?"

"I've looked after him," Mannering said pleasantly.
"Hallo, Betsy—everything's fixed. I'm staying at Nether
Manor too, so I'll take you there."

"Oh, *thank* you!" Betsy's eyes showed her relief.

They drove for ten minutes along the winding road,
then turned left into a tree-lined, private drive. The
sweep of meadowland beyond was just visible in the fail-
ing light. Straight ahead a house stood dark against the
afterglow, lights shining at many windows.

"If you'd drop me here, sir," Betsy said, "I could run
round to the back."

35

"All right, Betsy. Go with her, will you?" Mannering said to the driver.

"Yes, sir."

In the gloaming, Mannering studied the lines of Nether Manor. He judged it to be early Georgian, noting the handsome pillared porch, the tall windows, each having white-painted shutters pinned back against the rose-red brick walls. Soon, the driver came back, and settled into his seat. He took some time to do it, as if a certain mental agitation were finding an outlet in physical movement.

"Excuse me if I'm speaking out of turn, sir," he said at last.

"What's worrying you?" asked Mannering.

"That man you brought away from the cottage."

"What about him?"

"He hadn't any *right* there, sir, had he?"

"I don't know," said Mannering slowly. "I doubt it. I want to know, and I intend to find out, exactly what he was doing."

"Shouldn't that be a matter for the police?" The taxi driver's face was shadowed, but something in the twist of his body as he sat there was both aggressive and stubborn. His voice had a stubborn edge, too. "He was tied up when you brought him out, wasn't he?"

"You didn't miss much, did you?" said Mannering lightly. "He *was* tied up and he shouldn't have been in the cottage as far as I know, but——"

"How do you know he wasn't the man who attacked the old woman?"

"I don't," Mannering answered. "I don't know why she was attacked, either. I came down here at her request because she said she needed my help. But I don't think she's in any danger while she's in hospital, and I'm helping in the best way I know how." He settled squarely in his seat. "How long have you had your taxi license?"

Startled, the man answered: "Thirteen years."

"So you know the Salisbury police fairly well?"

"I know them, all right, and I've always been on good terms with them. I don't intend to risk——"

Mannering interrupted him. "I want you to take that package straight to their local headquarters—in Wilton Road, isn't it? Tell them I asked you to leave it in their care. Here's my card," he added. "Someone at the police station will know of me. And say I hope to be in Salisbury to pick up the package tomorrow or the day after."

As Mannering spoke, the driver's manner changed, his aggression fading.

"I'll certainly do *that*, sir!"

"And don't stop on the way," Mannering advised.

"I won't, sir!"

"Now we'll go up to the house," Mannering said.

The driver let in the clutch and drove round the circular carriageway to the front door. Mannering prepared to jump out of the car.

"How much do I owe you?"

"Time *and* distance, sir, one pound fifteen shillings."

Mannering gave the man two pounds ten shillings. "I may want you tomorrow," he told him. "Have you a card?" He took the printed card offered to him and went up to the house. The driver started his engine again as the front door was opened by an elderly manservant.

"Good evening, sir."

"I believe Colonel Cunliffe is expecting me—my name is Mannering, John Mannering."

"Oh yes, sir." The man, not unlike Larraby in appearance, stood to one side. "The Colonel asked me to show you straight to your room, sir. He is looking forward to seeing you at dinner."

Mannering nodded. "Thank you." It was puzzling he thought, that neither Cunliffe nor his daughter was here to make him welcome.

He followed the old man up a curving staircase with a beautiful polished balustrade, the walls hung with por-

37

traits. Staircase, hall and landing were fitted with precious things which struck an immediate chord in Mannering. He could soon be at home in this place. He was always at peace in a house where there was obvious reverence for the arts and culture of past days, and as he looked about him, all sense of urgency vanished. He would discover the truth about the paintings in good time; for the rest of the evening he could relax.

The thought was hardly in his mind when he heard a woman cry: "No, no, you mustn't!"

A man replied in a hard, carrying voice: "You are out of your senses. Of course I shall."

"It's been a beautiful day, sir, beautiful," babbled the manservant, his voice pitched overloud, in an attempt to drown the speakers. "This way, sir."

He ushered Mannering into a recess from which led two doors opposite each other, opened that on the right, and stood aside. Mannering entered a long, high-ceilinged room, with tall windows. A light sprayed over a deep armchair and a large canopied four-poster bed. In one corner was another doorway.

"The bathroom is there, sir. Dinner is at half-past nine. If there is anything you want, please ring."

"Thank you," Mannering said.

The man went out.

The first thing Mannering wanted was to know what the man and woman, whose voices he had overheard, were quarrelling about. He felt sure that the woman was Joanna, and could only guess that the man was her father. He hesitated. As a guest, the idea of eavesdropping was repellent, but there was much mystery here—and the old woman *had* been gravely injured. All thought and hope of relaxation had now gone.

He opened the bedroom door and stepped on to the landing. From there he glanced down into the well of the hall, saw that it was empty and walked quickly to the room where the couple were talking.

The man was saying: ". . . I simply don't understand you. Have you no pride in your heritage, Joanna? No pride in maintaining the family tradition? You can't be serious."

With a catch in her voice the girl replied: "I've never been more serious in my life. Please do as I ask, Daddy. *Please.*"

Mannering wished he were in the room and could see as well as hear what was going on. He could imagine the pleading on Joanna's face, the supplication in her eyes, but he had no idea at all of what Cunliffe looked like. Silence fell, and the impulse to open the door was almost overwhelming; it became greater as the silence lengthened. Mannerg moved closer, listening intently for Cunliffe's reply, but could hear nothing.

Suddenly the silence was broken by the sound of a woman's violent crying—and at the same time a man stepped across the hall below, his footsteps now sharp on polished marquetry, now softened by rich carpets.

CHAPTER FIVE

SHOCK AT DINNER

Mannering moved swiftly from the door, and went thoughtfully back to his room. What was it Joanna so desperately wanted her father to do, he wondered, and why should Colonel Cunliffe accuse his daughter of lack of family pride? As he turned into his own room a clock in the hall began to chime; it was nine o'clock. He found his case opened on the bed, and everything he needed in the bathroom; so someone knew he had been out of the room and could have seen him at the other door.

He had a quick bath, dressed, and was ready by twenty-five past nine. As he left his room he heard Cunliffe's voice again, this time downstairs.

"Now don't be long, Violet."

"Only a moment," a woman said. She appeared at a doorway and hurried towards the foot of the stairs, a tall, handsome woman in her middle forties. She stopped at the sight of Mannering, only a few steps above her.

"Oh, Mr. Mannering." Cunliffe appeared from the same doorway. "I'm so sorry I wasn't here when you arrived. Violet, may I present Mr. Mannering? Mr. Mannering, my sister, Lady Markly."

Violet Markly had a pleasant face and a friendly smile.

40

She murmured a conventional greeting and hurried up the stairs.

Cunliffe moved quietly across the hall with conventional ease. There was nothing in his manner to suggest anxiety or concern as he led the way to a small room where bottles gleamed on a dark chiffonier. Beyond, through an arched doorway, was a large dining-room, lit with candles in imposing silver candelabra.

"What will you have?" Cunliffe asked. "Violet said she'd only be a moment, which means ten minutes at least, and my daughter Joanna will be a little late." He hovered in front of the bottles.

"May I have a whisky and soda?"

Cunliffe poured out. "You've met my daughter, of course—your very good health—at the scene of the fire, she tells me. What a lot of excitement for an isolated place like this! The cottage was burned right down, I understand. Perhaps that attack on poor Eliza Doze saved her from a still more horrible fate. A shocking thing though, really shocking. Don't know what the country's coming to; even an old woman of nearly eighty isn't safe from these brutes. I wonder——"

"Do you know how she is?" interrupted Mannering.

"Oh, yes. Had a word with the hospital ten minutes ago; Joanna was very concerned. She's not badly hurt—nothing broken—and apparently she'll be up and about in a few days. How long are you going to be down here, Mannering?"

"Only a day or two," Mannering answered.

"Came by taxi, I understand. We've a little Mini. You can use it if it's any help—my daughter Hester's, but she's in London most of the time and won't drive up there. Parking problems. Understand you're in antiques."

"And paintings," observed Mannering, solemnly.

"Oh, yes, of course, paintings. I've some fine portraits here—a Gainsborough, a Breughel, a Vermeer, a Rubens . . ." The listing of his treasures ceased suddenly as Joanna came into the room.

She looked several years older than she had in jeans; but a lovely young woman. Her hair was piled high on her head, showing small, aristocratic ears, charmingly jewelled, and her make-up had been applied with care.

"Daddy, forgive me if I'm late . . . Mr. Mannering, lovely to see you again . . . Could I have a gin and It, Daddy? Not *too* much gin." She waited until her father had turned away, and then whispered in a voice Mannering could only just hear: "*Please don't show surprise at anything.*" With scarcely a pause she talked on in the normal voice of verbal intercourse, about the fire and the attack.

A few minutes later Lady Markly appeared, and they went in to dinner.

Even as versed as Mannering was at disguising his feelings, he could scarcely control a start of surprise; for the footman holding back Lady Markly's chair was Harry Anstiss.

It was a well-cooked meal, beautifully served, and Mannering ate and drank with concentration and pleasure, taking no more notice of Anstiss than Anstiss was taking of him.

Once the subject of the village sensation was over, the conversation drifted sparklingly to politics, motoring, yachting and finally to antiques. All three were knowledgeable, Joanna more than her aunt but less than her father. Mannering told them the story of the find in the Upper Amazon.

"And will you go, Mr. Mannering?" Lady Markly asked.

"I hope to," Mannering said.

He happened to be glancing at Anstiss as he spoke, and

could have sworn that Anstiss mouthed three words: "*You'll be lucky.*"

"A cigar, Mannering?" Cunliffe proffered a box when the men were alone with the port between them.

"Thank you."

"Going well? . . . Good. Now!" Cunliffe braced himself and looked squarely across the table. "Mannering, forgive me taking advantage of your visit here, but I've a problem. Can I speak in absolute confidence?"

Mannering nodded.

"I have your word?"

"You have my word."

Cunliffe watched Mannering intently.

"You—ah—you *have* been consulted on art thefts by the Yard, haven't you?"

"Occasionally, yes," said Mannering cautiously.

"I've a deuced strange problem on my hands, Mannering. Don't want to go to the police with it until I know the basic situation. You—ah—you've noticed my paintings? Oh, of course, we talked about them. Yes—I ah, have a small collection in the north gallery. Small but quite beautiful, and particularly valuable to me for sentimental reasons. They—ah—were stolen last week."

Mannering managed to put a note of astonishment into his voice.

"Stolen! A *week* ago?"

"Within the last week, certainly. I don't often go up to the north gallery, but did so seven days ago when everything was in order. I visited it again today, and this time noticed that a frame of the Rubens was scratched, took a closer look, and——" Cunliffe threw up his hands. "Copies! No doubt at all. *Copies!* I went through the lot, Mannering. Someone had taken the originals out of their frames and put in the copies. Damned good, mind you, would have fooled me but for the scratches on the frame. Care to see them?"

43

"Very much indeed," said Mannering.

Cunliffe glanced towards the door. "Joanna and Violet will find plenty to talk about for twenty minutes. Come this way, will you?"

There was another doorway leading from the dining-room, near which was a secondary staircase, spiraling upwards, the sides exquisitely carved. Cunliffe and Mannering walked up it, footsteps ringing on the solid oak. At the top was a long, narrow gallery which overlooked a part of the house which Mannering hadn't seen. One light glowed dimly from the ceiling, but Cunliffe switched on others, over each of the seven pictures, so placed to show them to their best advantage and to ensure that no direct light was reflected from the varnished surfaces.

Mannering's heart began to beat very fast, for these appeared to be identical with those he had brought from the cottage. He saw the Vermeer first, then the Breughel. In this light the copies, if indeed they were copies, were masterfully done.

"What do you make of them?" Cunliffe asked.

"I'd need special light and a special glass to be sure," Mannering said.

"Oh, these are copies all right," Cunliffe insisted, then went on uneasily: "I particularly don't want the police brought in, Mannering. On the other hand, I must know what happened to those paintings. It shouldn't be too difficult—after all, someone had to be up here for a considerable time. The door to the gallery is always kept locked, and the windows are impregnable. Impregnable. If a member of the staff—ah—or even one of the *family*, was remotely involved——" He broke off. "I'm sure you understand," he added.

"I do indeed," Mannering said.

"Will you help?"

"To find the thief?"

44

"Yes. *And* the paintings, dammit."

"Do you really believe this could be a family matter?" Mannering asked bluntly.

Cunliffe pursed his lips.

"I can only say that I must insist on not making the facts public, at least for the time being."

"Are the paintings insured?"

"Of course, Mannering. They are very valuable indeed."

"Unless you report the loss at once the insurance company might argue that you lost an opportunity to recover them, and dispute your claim," Mannering said.

Cunliffe's mouth dropped open.

"Seriously?"

"*Very* seriously."

"That—that certainly does put a different complexion on the matter," Cunliffe admitted. "I—ah—will have to give it a lot more consideration. Presumably it can keep until morning."

"Oh, yes. And you can say you told me and I advised waiting for a few hours," Mannering offered.

"Very thoughtful of you. You can understand how worried I am, can't you?"

"Yes, indeed," Mannering said again.

"Now—perhaps we ought to join the others." Cunliffe, still preoccupied, turned towards the head of the stairs and stood aside for Mannering to pass.

"I'd like to slip along to my room first," Mannering said.

"Of course. Of course. You can find your own way down, can't you?"

Mannering nodded. He watched Cunliffe go downstairs, then walked swiftly along the corridor. Reaching his bedroom, he paused for a moment, then swung the door sharply back against the wall, half expecting someone to be lurking behind it. But the room was empty.

The bedclothes had been turned down, otherwise everything seemed to be exactly as it had been before. He studied the room more closely. Now he noticed that two drawers stood out more than he recalled, and he thought a chair had been pushed to one side. Cautiously, he went to the bathroom.

It was empty.

There was no way of being sure that the room had been searched, but almost certainly Anstiss would have taken any chance to look for the paintings. Mannering went out and down the stairs. Cunliffe and Lady Markly were sitting in front of a television set from the screen of which a black face shone, a deep voice sounded. Mannering heard the word "Commonwealth" before Cunliffe switched off.

"Don't do that for me," Mannering said.

"Oh, nothing worth seeing tonight," said Cunliffe bluffly. "My daughter's gone to bed, Mannering—very tired. She asked me to wish you goodnight for her."

"And I must be off," Lady Markly said. "I live in a cottage in the grounds, Mr. Mannering."

"May I walk there with you?"

"Really, there's no need."

"Be a very good idea," Cunliffe said. (Was it his imagination, wondered Mannering, or was his host anxious to get rid of him?) "So many odd things seem to have happened recently. And it's a very dark night."

It was indeed a very dark night, despite the brightness of the stars. The pale outline of the carriageway showed up eerily. Beyond the trees, lights showed at windows.

"That's the cottage, Mr. Mannering; not very far, you see."

"Far enough on a dark night," Mannering answered.

That was when he thought he heard a sound behind them, but he did not turn round. He talked in pleasantries until he and Lady Markly reached the cottage gate, where they said goodnight. Mannering waited until she was safely inside, then turned back to the main house. He had not taken a dozen steps before he heard faint footfalls behind him. Now he had no doubt at all that he was being followed.

CHAPTER SIX

THE THREATS

Mannering did not alter his pace as he made his way back towards the Manor. He was acutely aware of the lights which suddenly flared out from the windows. He could not have been more vulnerable.

The footsteps continued.

Were there two men? Or just one? Was it Anstiss? With this uncertainty for company, Mannering had a vivid mental picture of Joanna Cunliffe as she had pleaded with him to let Anstiss go.

Why had she done so?

He was halfway between the cottage and the house, when several of the lights of the house went out. That helped a little. And whoever was behind him seemed to keep at a fair distance. But surely no one would follow him simply for the sake of seeing where he went?

Suddenly, startlingly, a man spoke.

"Stop there, Mannering."

Mannering went on.

"Stop there if you don't want a bullet in your back." The voice was low-pitched and clear; he thought it was Anstiss but was not sure.

A shot would be heard, and with so many people about

someone would be bound to investigate. Mannering went on but he clenched his teeth.

"I've warned you," the man behind him said; it *was* Anstiss. And now he seemed to be drawing nearer.

The threat to shoot was probably made to unnerve Mannering and to make him more vulnerable to some other form of attack. How would it come? Anstiss was a small man, but he might well carry a cosh or a stick, and he could leap forward and smash a blow down on Mannering's head. Mannering keyed himself. If he ran he could reach the safety of the house—unless Anstiss did have a gun. But that would lose another chance of questioning the man. If he spun round and attacked . . .

A second man spoke out of the darkness on his right.

"Stop there, Mannering."

Mannering turned his head and saw a vague, dark shape, the pale blur of a face, and as he did so heard the man behind him running, sensed the moment when Anstiss leapt at him. He leaned forward, bending almost double, and Anstiss went flying over his shoulders. On the instant Mannering jumped towards the dark shape—the shape of a man—of a big man.

They collided.

The shock of the impact sent Mannering reeling back, sent the other staggering too. He was both big and heavy, and if youth were on his side, would have all the advantages. Mannering guessed that Anstiss would soon attack again; the obviously sensible thing was to run for the house. But even as the thought flashed through his mind, Mannering saw the big man clearly, judged his position and leapt forward, arms outstretched to grab his ankles and to pull him down. His hands opened and closed, and the man pitched backwards, leaving Mannering stretched on the ground at full length. Before he could start to get up, Anstiss leapt.

Mannering felt a kick in the side, another on the shoulder. The next moment he was struck savagely on the back of the head. Senses reeling, he tried to struggle to his feet, but another blow fell with the weight of a sledge-hammer, and he lost consciousness.

"Watch him," muttered Anstiss.

The other man shrugged. "He's dead to the world."

"He could be foxing."

"Don't you believe it. Take his arms."

Warily, Anstiss moved towards Mannering's head, bending down and gripping his arms as the other took his legs. They lifted him, sagging in the middle, and carried him away from the drive and the lawns. Before they had gone fifty yards, Anstiss gasped:

"I must rest."

"Just a breather."

"How far do we have to go?"

" 'Nother hundred yards."

Twice more they lowered Mannering as they carried him through the trees towards a small hut. They were both gasping for breath when they reached it, dropped Mannering and opened the door. It made little sound. The big man went inside, flashing a torch, the beam falling on saws, a scything machine, ropes, canvas bags and two wire-netted cages half full of leaves. Anstiss followed him, and lit an oil lamp. There was only one window and a piece of sacking hung from it. Along one wall was a garden bench, with a broken arm rest.

"Put him on that," the big man said. "Get a move on."

When Mannering had fallen, the jolt had brought him back to consciousness. He was vaguely aware of the light inside the hut, but his head ached, and his body was too limp for him to make any effort to get away. He saw the men come out of the doorway, dark against the dim light, and closed his eyes. They picked him up again and carried him inside; he steeled himself against the pain of being dropped, but this time they placed him on the bench, his head at one end, his legs resting over the broken rail at the other. Then they sat down, one on an upturned drum, one on a coil of rope. There was a smell of oil, of new-mown grass, of decomposing leaves—and freshly, of tobacco smoke.

The big man looked at his companion. "You sure he brought them away?"

"He *must* have done."

"You didn't *see* him with them."

"No, but——"

"So they *could* have gone up in smoke." The man's voice was coarse, but he spoke with authority while Anstiss was on the defensive.

"He wouldn't let them burn—not Mannering."

"He let the cottage burn."

Anstiss sounded almost desperate. "What's the matter with you? I put the petrol up there and started the rags smouldering; no one could stop the place going up in smoke. What are you getting at, Lobb?"

Lobb.

The big man spoke with great deliberation. "If *he* didn't take the paintings, who did?"

"But he must have taken them. There was no one else."

"No one?" asked Lobb, coldly.

There was a long silence, followed by a belated gasp from Anstiss.

"Are you suggesting *I* took them?"

"I'm asking who did, if Mannering didn't?"

"I'm not a double-crosser!"

"I hope not," said Lobb quietly. "It would go hard on anyone who double-crossed me, Annie, and don't you forget it." After another pause, Mannering heard a stirring of movement as if the big man were getting up. "Let's see if he's awake," he added, in the same laconic yet menacing way.

Mannering, now fully conscious, sensed that the man was approaching stealthily and sensed the viciousness in his tone. He opened his eyes a fraction. Lobb was drawing at a cigarette and making it glow very red.

Taking the cigarette from his lips, he began to lower it. Through his lashes, Mannering could see the way his thin mouth was twisting, had the impression that the prospect of what he was about to do gave Lobb real pleasure.

Mannering waited until the cigarette was only six inches above his forehead, then shot his right arm up, clenching the other's wrist in a vicious twist. Lobb keapt in the air with surprise and pain, cannoned into Anstiss and they both went sprawling. Mannering swung himself off the bench, snatched up a moss rake and thrust it against Lobb's chest, pinning Anstiss beneath him. Wriggling free, Anstiss jumped for the door, but Mannering, driven by a sense of desperation and knowing that he must win, caught him and flung him against the wall. Thinking and acting with controlled speed, he picked up a coil of rope. Standing over the men he made a noose and, almost in the same movement, dropped it over Anstiss's shoulders.

"No!" shrieked Anstiss. "Don't—don't hang . . . !"

Mannering jerked the rope down as far as his elbows, inch by inch, and drew it tight, made a double knot, then wound the end of the rope round a big hook in the wall. All the time he kept watch on Lobb, who was slowly recovering but still nursing his wrist. The expression in his eyes warned Mannering, who saw him move stealthily towards a scythe, its blade glistening from recent use. Mannering swung round, pushing the rake against his chest.

"Touch that scythe and I'll claw your face with this."

Lobb went still.

He was a powerful, ruggedly good-looking man, with

attractive curly hair, pale gray eyes and a square chin with a deep cleft. Only his thin mouth spoiled him. He was dressed in a thick, knee-length coat, open at the neck to show a collar and tie. Despite his stillness, there was no fear in his gaze, only wariness.

"Get in the corner behind that mowing machine," Mannering ordered.

Lobb didn't move.

"*Now,*" Mannering said, very softly and he drew the rake through the air, inches from Lobb's face. Lobb glanced towards the machine, half turned as if to go for it, then grabbed the handle of the rake just above the prongs and pulled savagely.

Mannering let the rake go. Lobb's strength was such that he pulled the head with great force against his neck, and for a moment must have been in agony. He dropped the rake. It clattered to the cement floor and Mannering stepped over it, took Lobb's right arm, twisted it behind him and thrust it upwards in a hammer-lock. Pushing his captive behind the mower, Mannering maneuvered the heavy machine so that Lobb couldn't get out without climbing over it. Then, back at the bench, he picked up the rake.

"Now, what were you saying?"

"My God," cried Lobb hoarsely, "I'll see you under the ground for this!"

"No doubt those are your amiable intentions; whether they're carried out or not is another matter. Who are you acting for?"

"If you think you can make me talk——"

"If I can't make you talk I can make sure you get three years for assault, five years if you've a record. Who pays you?"

"I pay myself."

"Lobb," said Mannering slowly, "I've only to open that door and shout, and I can have the police here in twenty minutes. Miss Joanna might have persuaded me to let Anstiss go, but no one will persuade me to let *you* go until I know what this is all about. Who pays you?"

The pale light gave Lobb's eyes a baleful gleam. He tightened his lips until they almost disappeared, and breathed heavily through his nostrils. Mannering sat back on the bench, ankles crossed, rake to hand. Startlingly through the quiet came the hooting of an owl.

"Made up your mind?" he asked at last.

"So you want to know who pays me," Lobb said harshly.

"I *mean* to know."

"Nobody pays me."

"That's true!" gasped Anstiss.

"I get what I can where I can find it and I sell to the highest bidder," said Lobb flatly. "You're in the trade, you don't need telling how many dealers and collectors will buy without asking questions. I'm my own boss."

"He *is*, at that!" cried Anstiss.

"And I use a lot of little men like Anstiss to do my running for me," Lobb went on. "They find out where the paintings are, I give them the once-over, and if I know where I can place them quickly, I buy. Anything else you want to know?"

"What makes you think you're a judge of paintings?"

"Fifteen years in the biggest gallery in Europe." Lobb gave a curiously one-sided grin. "I was an art student at the Slade, I was at the Beaux Arts in Paris, I can copy nearly everything anyone puts down on canvas, but it's hard work. I got tired of doing copies for a pittance while other men made fortunes out of them, so I went into the business myself. Don't make any mistake, Mannering. I know paintings; I'm an expert. Got a job for me at Quinns?" The grin became a leer. "And I'm not an old lag, like your manager Larraby."

If he knew that about Larraby, how much more did he know? Mannering wondered.

"He's telling you the gospel truth," Anstiss muttered.

"Who do you want Colonel Cunliffe's paintings for?"

"No one special," said Lobb. He straightened up and there was boldness in his manner. "How about an even split, Mannering?"

Mannering didn't answer.

"Don't tell me you're as honest as they say you are," Lobb jeered. "Otherwise, what brought you down to look over that old woman's paintings?" When Mannering still did not answer, Lobb went on: "Shy of committing yourself?"

"Which of you attacked Eliza Doze?" demanded Mannering coldly.

"I didn't mean to hurt her, just put the wind up her," babbled Anstiss. "I wouldn't have touched her if she hadn't come for me with a poker; it was self-defense, really, that's what it was—self defense."

"What was the idea?" asked Mannering. "Steal the paintings and then set fire to the place and pretend everything was destroyed?"

"Now why should we do that?" sneered Lobb.

"For insurance," said Mannering.

"He's bright, Mannering is," said Lobb. "The only one who'd get the insurance money would be the Colonel; where would *I* come in?" He gave a snort of a laugh, and glanced at Anstiss almost gloatingly. "He doesn't know, see? I told you he didn't. Okay, Mannering, we've talked enough. Hand over the paintings and go back to London and I'll let bygones be bygones. Make any more trouble and the first thing I'll do is prove it was *Miss Joanna* who stole those pictures. Make a nice juicy scandal, wouldn't it? Take it from me, if *I* go to jail, she will too." When Mannering said nothing, he went on: "I'll do a deal. I'll pay you twenty-five per cent of the proceeds. How about it, Mannering?"

CHAPTER SEVEN

THIEF?

If Joanna had stolen the paintings, this would explain much that was mysterious about her behavior. But why should she steal them?

Mannering could not be sure that Lobb had told him the truth, but they couldn't stay here all night. Either he had to send for the police and charge the two men, or he had to let them go. Given half a chance, Lobb would try to make him give up the missing paintings, would use any method in his attempt, but that was a risk Mannering was prepared to take.

He was committed to Cunliffe, too. If he went to the police now, the whole story would come out.

"How do you know Miss Joanna took the paintings?" he demanded.

"She told me so," Lobb asserted, jeeringly.

"Told you?"

"That's right, Mannering—she told me."

"How did she know you might be interested?"

Lobb laughed. "You'd be surprised how many people know me. I knew she needed money so I got the message through to her." There was a sneer in his voice all the time. "Want to shop her, Mannering?"

Mannering thought quickly. He was obviously going

to get little, if any, further information from Lobb, and none at all from Anstiss; and if he turned the two men over to the police, that would involve breaking his promise to Colonel Cunliffe.

Still holding the rake, he got to his feet and moved towards the door. Then he turned to Lobb.

"I should like you and your friend to stay here for ten minutes. If you make any attempt to catch up with me, then I shall hand the pictures *and* you and Anstiss over to the police. Is that understood?"

Slowly, he leaned the rake against the wall, and went out into the night, conscious of the stare from two pairs of eyes. As he closed the door the owl hooted again. Through the trees he could see some lights at the Manor; it would not have surprised him had Cunliffe sent someone to look for him, but no one was about. He reached the pale gravel of the path and stepped out briskly towards the house. Soon he was ringing the bell at the front door. Almost immediately the elderly manservant opened it; obviously he had been waiting. He looked very tired.

"Did I keep you up?" Mannering asked.

"It's quite all right, sir."

But he chained and bolted the door as Mannering crossed the hall.

Mannering looked into the room in which he and Colonel Cunliffe and Joanna had talked before dinner, but it was empty. At any other time he would have been surprised by Cunliffe's neglect even of an unexpected guest; now, he decided to go up to his own room. As he reached the foot of the main staircase, however, Cunliffe appeared at the balustrade.

"My dear Mannering, I'm so sorry. Shall I come down or will you join me in my study? Ah—capital," he continued, as Mannering went upstairs. "The police telephoned you," he added, a shade apprehensively.

"The Yard?" asked Mannering, surprised.

"No, the Salisbury chaps. They want you to call them back—a Chief Inspector Fishlock." He led Mannering into a large, book-lined room, and Mannering looked about him appreciatively. "Would you care to use this telephone? And how about a night-cap? Or if you'd prefer coffee . . . ?" He left the sentence in mid-air.

"A brandy would be very pleasant," Mannering said. He reached the telephone and saw a note: *Will Mr. Mannering please telephone Salisbury* 12121. Cunliffe busied himself at a corner cupboard as Mannering dialed the number and asked for Chief Inspector Fishlock.

"Fishlock speaking," a man said in a brisk voice.

"My name is Mannering."

"Oh, yes, Mr. Mannering. Thank you for calling." Fishlock spoke in a businesslike manner. "A taxi driver named Arnold brought in a parcel which he said you asked him to hand to us."

"That's quite correct," Mannering agreed.

"Is it lost property, Mr. Mannering?"

"I'd like you to hold it until I come for it," Mannering said. "I'd no place to put it here in Salisbury and the banks were shut. If you care to telephone Scotland Yard . . ."

"Oh, we know who you *are*," Chief Inspector Fishlock. "But it isn't customary for us to keep any parcel or package here without opening it and checking the contents."

"Do that if you wish," Mannering told him. "Only don't disclose the nature of the contents to anyone, will you? I think I came across a rare discovery in Salisbury."

"I see, sir. Well, no names, no pack-drill, if you know what I mean—but we should hate a gentleman of your reputation to come down here and be cheated."

"You wouldn't hate it more than I would," Mannering said drily.

Fishlock chuckled dutifully, and wished Mannering goodnight.

58

Cunliffe had gone into a small ante-room, but appeared almost as soon as Mannering replaced the receiver, bringing brandy in a glass big enough for Mannering to cup with both hands. He sniffed the bouquet appreciatively, while studying his host. Possibly due to his preoccupation with his own affairs, Cunliffe did not appear to have realized how long Mannering had been out, nor that his shoes were muddied and that his clothes were rumpled.

"I've given a lot of thought to the problem of the missing paintings," Cunliffe said. "Mr. Mannering, if I ask the insurance company to accept *you* as the official investigator, not the police, do you think they would agree?"

"Probably."

"And would *you* agree?"

"I don't see why not."

"Thank you," said Cunliffe, with great relief. "I really am most grateful. And now, is there anything I can do to help?"

Mannering nodded. "Are there photographs of the missing paintings?" he asked.

"Oh, yes, photographs in colour and a full description of each. I had a number of copies made some years ago, for the family and a few close friends. When would you like them? Tonight?"

"If it possible?"

"Of course. Excuse me for a moment." Cunliffe went into the ante-room again leaving Mannering to think over his encounter with Lobb and Anstiss. Taking everything into account, Mannering felt that so far the edge was with, rather than against him.

A few minutes later Cunliffe returned. "Here we are!" He put a beautifully tooled leather volume into Mannering's hands. "I don't want to sentimentalize, Mannering, but these seven paintings do have a very great personal value for me. Their loss would be . . ." He broke off.

"I quite understand," Mannering said. "I'll do everything I can to get them back."

"You're very kind," Cunliffe said. "Very kind. And it *will* be entirely confidential?"

"As I've promised," Mannering assured him.

Twenty minutes later, with murmured apologies and renewed thanks, Cunliffe retired to bed. Outside his own room Mannering hesitated for a few seconds, then opened the door very cautiously.

There was no need for caution; no one was there. He had not really expected anyone, and yet . . .

He examined the window, and saw that he could secure it so as to have it open a few inches without the slightest risk of anyone getting in. He checked the door and locked and bolted it, checked the bathroom, and felt assured that no one could enter that way, either. At least he could rest in peace tonight.

And he was exhausted!

He undressed quickly, got into a hot bath, soaked for ten minutes to ease the stiffness he was beginning to feel after his exertions with Lobb and Anstiss, and was in bed within a quarter of an hour of getting out. Visions of all that had happened passed hazily before him, and the roaring of the fire at the cottage seemed to echo through his mind. It was odd that he had met so many strange people, yet not the old woman he had specifically come to see.

Eliza Doze . . .

Doze, Doze, Doze . . . doze, doze doze . . .

He drifted into sleep, warm, snug, the ache seeping out of him.

He slept . . .

And he became aware of something, someone, touching him, of a hand at his mouth, at his head. He did not start, for waking had come gradually, and now every faculty was alert.

"Mr. Mannering!" It was the voice of Joanna, whispering. "Mr. Mannering!"

Joanna's hand was over his mouth to prevent him from

crying out, Joanna's other hand was at his forehead, as if to soothe him. Her lips were very close to his hear. "Mr. Mannering, wake up."

He spoke quietly. "What is it, Joanna?"

She started back, violently.

"You're awake!"

"Not with intent," Mannering said. "What is it?"

She took her hands away and moved from the bed. She wore a dressing-gown of some light-colored material, over a filmy nightdress. It could not have been chosen more cleverly to show the girl at her most seductive.

Seductive?

"Mr. Mannering," she repeated in that pleading voice, "*please* listen to me."

Mannering sat up. "I'll listen." He arranged a pillow to his greater comfort, and studied her. He could not rid himself of the feeling that her diaphanous covering had been arranged deliberately, as part of an act. Yet she looked too young, too innocent, to behave in such a way.

"You have those paintings, haven't you?"

"What paintings?" Mannering asked.

"Must you pretend? The ones from the cottage, of course."

"Or from the north gallery," Mannering suggested.

"From—the cottage. You went there and took them from—Anstiss. I know you did."

"I took them away from the cottage," Mannering agreed.

"You must let me have them."

"You—or Anstiss?"

"You must let me have them," she repeated. "They're not yours, you've no right to them."

"I've more right than Anstiss or Lobb," Mannering said, drily.

"You haven't, they . . ."

Mannering interrupted her. "If they're the paintings from the north gallery I've every right to keep them.

Your father has asked me to try to get them back for him."

She closed her eyes and seemed to sway, first backwards, then towards him. She leaned against the bed, very close to him, and peered into his eyes.

"They're *mine*," she said huskily. "They were my mother's, and when father dies they'll be mine. I've more right to them than anybody. Please let me have them."

"Joanna," Mannering said firmly, "I have been commissioned by your father to find them for him, and if I give them to anyone it will be to him. Supposing you go back to bed—and in the morning tell me what this is all about."

"They're *mine*," she repeated.

"Joanna . . ."

"They're mine and I want them," she said hoarsely. "And I'm going to get them. Where are they?"

"In a safe place."

"They're not in this room because I——" She broke off.

"So you were the searcher," said Mannering drily. "No, I don't leave valuables in the expected places, Joanna."

"If you don't let me have them I'll tear my clothes off and jump on you and *scream!*" she cried. "I'll scream until the whole household is awake, and I'll say you tried to rape me. I mean it! Give me those paintings!"

CHAPTER EIGHT

THE AMATEUR WANTON

Joanna did mean it.

Mannering, taken aback by the unexpectedness of her threat, was amused for an instant, and smiled—realizing at once what a mistake this was. Joanna drew a deep, shuddering breath. Clenching her fists, she shook them in his face.

"Don't dare laugh at me! I'll scream the place down; I'll get everyone in here; my father will horsewhip you!"

Her father might, with advantage, Mannering thought, have spanked her more often than he had.

"Give me those pictures. Tell me where they are!" Her whole body was aquiver; in her fear-inspired rage she must have been oblivious of her look of wantonness. "I mean what I say, I'll scream the place down."

"If you must, you must," Mannering said, "but be quick, I'm tired out already running after your pictures."

"If I scream——"

"Go ahead, Joanna. *Scream!* Or perhaps I ought to do the screaming," Mannering suggested. "After all, I'm the victim."

She was so taken aback that she could only stand and stare.

"Or else go back to bed," Mannering said.

Joanna caught her breath.

"You—you know what will happen if I *do* scream?"

"Do *you* know that if an attractive young girl is found in a man's room wearing her nightclothes, she'll be branded as a hussy?" Mannering asked. "Now if *I'd* broken into *your* room ——" He stopped short. "*Wait* a minute. How did you get in?"

"The door was open."

"It wasn't——" Mannering began, then broke off, struck first by a sense almost of shock that he should have been sleeping so unguardedly in a room into which it was so easy to force entry; secondly, by realization that Joanna was in a state of extreme tension and that she was in deep need of help. What he must do, thought Mannering, was try to ease that tension, and so make her more likely to tell him what the trouble was. He leaned back, relaxed, and changed the whole tone of his voice. "What's the problem, Joanna?" he asked. "Can I help?"

"You—you can help by giving me those paintings!"

"I think that would only make more trouble for you," Mannering said. "What *is* worrying you, Joanna?"

"I—I just want those paintings. They *are* mine."

"I don't think your father would agree," Mannering said. "Shall we call him and talk it over with him?"

"No!"

"What have you done that you don't want him to know about?"

"Nothing! I just want the paintings."

"Joanna," Mannering said, "Eliza Doze was seriously injured because someone wanted the paintings. I was attacked in the grounds tonight and very nearly tortured because someone wanted the paintings."

"*Tortured?* I—I don't believe it."

"You should, because it's true. What's Anstiss doing here as a footman?"

"He—he works here."

"How long is it since he came?"

"Only a week. He—he's a *good* footman."

"I don't doubt it. He's not a very good thief."

"He wouldn't torture . . ."

"Not Anstiss. Lobb."

"Lobb!" exclaimed Joanna in an anguished tone. For a moment Mannering thought she was going to collapse and he moved quickly to support her, but she recovered. "If you've met Lobb," she went on through clenched teeth, "then you know how serious it is."

"Joanna—what are you being blackmailed about?" Mannering asked quietly. "You can tell me; I'll promise to keep that a secret, at least."

"Blackmailed," she echoed in a whisper. "I'm not being blackmailed. You—you're mad. You're mad!" She backed towards the door and then stood with both arms stretched out in supplication. "Can't you *see* how important it is to me? While to you it can't matter at all. *Where are they?*"

"Joanna," Mannering said quietly, "if you tell me the whole story and I really believe that you should have the paintings, I'll see that you get them."

"I—I can't tell you."

"Then you can't have them. What were they doing at Eliza Doze's cottage, anyhow?"

Joanna didn't answer, but stood there, tears misting her eyes. Slowly she dropped her arms to her side and turned away. Each movement was so slow, so deliberate, that Mannering suspected she hoped at the last moment he would relent. She opened the door—which he had locked and bolted—and went out slowly.

Mannering did not move.

The door closed with a faint click. He watched the handle, still gripped from the further side. The temptation to go and open the door, to start reasoning with her again, was almost overwhelming, but he stayed where he was.

Would she, herself, open the door and make a fresh appeal?

The handle turned, then went still. There was no sound of movement at all, but he could imagine her going very slowly along the passage towards her room, head bowed, shoulders drooping. *Was* she as distressed and troubled as she seemed? Or was there some degree of duplicity, of pretence? He couldn't be sure. He wanted to believe in her, but could not entirely do so.

Should he go after her?

"Nonsense!" he exclaimed aloud, and then glanced up at the bolt of the door and at the key. How had she come in? Had it been a comparatively simple matter of forcing a lock he could have understood—but who had the skill and dexterity to force a *bolt* from the outside?

His lips twisted wryly.

He had.

There were far-off days when he had been the Baron, jewel-thief and cracksman extraordinary, a Robin Hood and Raffles of a man. Then, with special tools and after great practice, he could have eased a bolt open, but not without leaving some sign that he had done so. He got out of bed and stepped across to the door, examining it closely. There were no scratches, no fresh marks of any kind.

With infinite care he eased the key out of the lock. It was an old-fashioned one, and the end could be gripped by a special shaped pair of pliers—but these would leave scratch marks at the top. There were none.

There were only two possibilities: one, that Joanna had been hiding in the room, and had unlocked and unbolted the door before waking him; two, and this was much more likely, that there was another, secret, way of entrance. He began to look around. The paneled walls were hung with tapestries, and one of these might well conceal . . .

A high-pitched scream pierced the silence of the

house. Mannering sprang instinctively to the door, hand outstretched, but suddenly drew back. Was this a trick? Was this Joanna's way of carrying out her threat?

Be damned to that!

He pulled open the door as another scream, loud and frightening, echoed through the hall and along the landing. A dim light glowed at the head of the stairs and in the hall itself. Mannering reached the landing as Colonel Cunliffe appeared.

Joanna, down below, cried: "No, no!"

A door slammed.

"What is it?" gasped Cunliffe.

Mannering rushed past him and down the stairs. There was a sobbing from somewhere out of sight, and as he reached the hall he saw Joanna. She was crouched on the floor, her body rocking to and fro, and if there were doubts of the genuineness of her mood before, there could be none now.

Scattered round about her were the fallen locks and strands of her dark hair.

Someone had hacked at it, as if with shears, so that pale gaps showed close to the scalp. There were patches which stood wildly on end, while others, still long, drooped over her hands.

Mannering raced towards the front door as Cunliffe ran to his daughter. The bolts and chains which the old servant had secured were now out of position. Mannering pulled the door open, and stared into the night. There was no moon; only the stars had brightness, but they gave little light down here.

Somewhere, a long way off, he thought he heard footsteps, but they stopped suddenly and then, sharp and clear, came the staccato noise of a motor-cycle engine, uneven at first, then purring into coherence as the machine gathered speed. There would be no chance at all of catching up with the rider.

Mannering turned to Joanna and her father.

Cunliffe was on one knee by the girl's side, in attempted comfort, but Joanna was still sobbing in that degree of grief and shock untouched by sympathy. To and fro her body rocked, to and fro.

"Mannering," Cunliffe asked helplessly, "what shall I do? What the devil shall I do?"

"Give her a sedative and get her back to bed," Mannering told him. "If you haven't anything stronger than aspirin, then a stiff brandy."

"Er—Violet has some tablets."

"Can we send for them?"

"Yes," Cunliffe muttered. "Yes." He looked up as two men appeared—one of them Anstiss, the other the old butler. "Anstiss, hurry over to Lady Markly and ask her if she will give you some of her sedative tablets. Hurry man! Don't just stand there."

"Yes, sir," said Anstiss hoarsely.

"What happened?" asked the old man, huskily. "Is—is Miss Joanna all right, sir?"

"Who would do such a thing?" muttered Cunliffe. He straightened up, grunting. "She—she doesn't seem to hear me."

"Let me carry her," Mannering offered.

He bent over the girl, put one arm behind her knees, another round her shoulders and lifted her; she was heavier than he had expected, a dead weight, without buoyancy.

"This way, sir," the old man said.

Mannering carried Joanna up the stairs and along a secondary passage, into a room on the right, Cunliffe following him. A bedside light was on, showing a pleasant room with wide, chintz-curtained windows. The bed had been turned down but not slept in that night. Mannering, breathing heavily, placed the girl down carefully. She was pale, and cold, and very still. A heavy lock of hair had been cut off above the forehead, and a scratch was bleeding slightly. That was the only sign of injury.

Mannering turned to Cunliffe. "I think you ought to call a doctor," he said abruptly. He did not like the girl's pallor or rigidity, and this shock on top of her emotional exhaustion might have grave consequences.

If he had only run at the sound of the first scream.

Nonsense, he told himself, I couldn't have prevented it; I didn't lose five seconds.

He had a sense of uneasiness all the same, almost of guilt. If he had gone to see what the girl had done, instead of worrying about how she had got into his room, he might have saved her from this terrifying experience.

Cunliffe was speaking into a telephone on the other side of the bed.

"Yes . . . Ask him to come at once, please . . . Thank you." He rang off.

She left my room and took her time going down the stairs, Mannering was thinking. Her attacker must have been waiting out of sight, but she kept free long enough to scream. It was the kind of viciousness he would have expected from Lobb, but why should he—why should *anyone*—do such a thing as this?

Cunliffe stood on the far side of the bed, looking down on his daughter. He raised his hands, then let them fall heavily by his side. The old butler, heavily buttressed in a plaid dressing-gown several sizes too big for him, brought in a silver tray, with brandy and three glasses. He glanced at Joanna.

"Did *you* see anything, Middleton?" asked Cunliffe.

"Nothing at all, sir, nothing." The butler put the tray down. "Who would do such a thing to Miss Joanna?" There were tears in his eyes and his voice was unsteady. "Is there anything more I can do, sir?"

"No—you go back to bed," Cunliffe said, and glanced at a clock by the telephone. "Half-past three." He spoke resignedly, as he poured out a drink. "Brandy, Mannering?"

"No thanks."

"Think we ought to give Joanna . . . ?"

"I'd leave it to the doctor," advised Mannering.

He waited until he heard Violet Markly's voice in the hall, and then went out. Anstiss was telling her, in shocked tones, what had happened. He gave Mannering a single half-scared, half-pleading look.

"I'll be in my room if I'm wanted," Mannering said.

He went back to his room, sat on the edge of the bed and stared at the door. He felt very tired; reaction from his own ordeal and from this second shock was setting in. Perhaps he should have had that brandy. He leaned back against the head of the bed, picturing Joanna in her anger and her fear. She had looked so beautiful, not least because of her lovely hair. He began to doze, and slowly the image faded. His head slid heavily down the bed panel, but he was too uncomfortable to go soundly to sleep.

He mustn't go to sleep; he must find out how Joanna had entered the room. He made himself get up, then went to the bathroom and splashed his face and hands with ice-cold water. Feeling better, he began to examine the walls. It seemed evident that there was a concealed door here—uncommon in Georgian houses but not unknown. Methodically he tapped the wall, moving the tapestries and the lighter pieces of furniture, but found nothing.

The ceiling had three big beams; it seemed solid enough.

He began to examine the floor. This would prove the longest task; he had to go down on his knees and check each board, especially those which had cracks or a join in them. If Joanna had come in through the floor, then a section presumably opened upwards; he took his penknife from the dressing-table, opened it at a skeleton-key blade and hooked board after board. It was a waste of time, of course; the girl must have been hiding under the bed, after all.

A board moved slightly; and creaked.

He pulled again, his interest quickening, and it came up far enough for him to get his fingers underneath. It was fastened to an adjoining board, a section of which was hinged so that it was like a hatch cover. Very slowly and cautiously he opened it as far as it would go.

CHAPTER NINE

THE STUDIO

The opening was two feet or so across one way and about eighteen inches the other. Below, it was pitch dark. Mannering moved across to the wardrobe, took a pencil torch out of his jacket pocket and came back. The light showed the outline of a narrow ladder, leading down out of sight. Mannering began to climb down the ladder, finding the glow of light from his bedroom less necessary as he became accustomed to the gloom. The ladder was firm, fastened to the wall of a cavity similar, though smaller, to a lift shaft. At each step he tested the rung cautiously, and when he had come down fifteen rungs, he touched ground.

Standing in near darkness, he shone the torch about him. Three walls were blank; the fourth had the outline of a narrow door. There was no handle, merely a recessed hole large enough for two fingers. He put his fingers into this and pulled.

The door yielded. Very slowly, he opened it. Darkness lay beyond, and stillness and silence—and the smell of oil paint. He shone the torch again, and the light fell upon an easel, a half-finished painting propped against a wall, a palette and a table littered with a mess of tubes of paint, mostly squeezed until they were half empty. Mannering shone the torch on to the other walls, and saw a light switch against a door on the right of the one through which he had entered.

He went across and pressed it down.

A fluorescent light flickered and then came on, almost as bright as day. It shone on a long, narrow room stacked with frames and parts of frames. A woodworker's bench carried a fair variety of tools, another bench was laden with tubes of paint, canvas and hardboard. Round the walls were modern paintings, attractive in their way but showing no great skill—and in one corner was an excellent copy of an early portrait by Franz Hals.

The room was, roughly, the same size as the north gallery, and Mannering guessed that it ran beneath it. Over in the far corner was a spiral staircase, the steps of wood, the balusters of beautifully worked wrought-iron. That must lead up to the gallery. Mannering took another swift look round, then switched off the light and went back to the door leading to the ladder. If Cunliffe or anyone else had come to his room during his absence, they would realise he had found the secret entrance to the studio.

He climbed back without difficulty, lowered the hatch and placed a heavy chair over it; now no one else could take him by surprise. Then he went across to the bed and lay down at full length; the relaxing of his body was exquisite relief.

Who was the artist?

Or rather—who were the artists? For judging by the difference in style and methods of work, there had been more than one painter in that studio. Was Lobb one of them? How could such a man obtain facilities to paint at Nether Manor? Did Cunliffe know about it? It was useless to speculate, and yet Mannering found himself doing so. Restlessly he got off the bed and went out on to the landing. There was no one about, but the main lights were still on, and from somewhere he heard voices. Joanna's room? He approached the closed door, and through it recognised the voice of Lady Markly.

"Just absolute quiet, then."

"Yes, Lady Markly—and if she doesn't show any improvement when she comes round, I think she should be put under observation at the Infirmary." The doctor had a high-pitched voice, giving Mannering the impression of a fussy man. "I'll telephone after surgery in the morning—and in the meantime, should you feel there's the slightest need, please send for me."

Mannering moved away as the voice drew nearer. The door opened and Cunliffe came out, followed by a middle-aged man with a very high forehead and pebble-lens glasses. There were signs in his apparel that he had been summoned hastily, and from bed.

"Goodnight, goodnight."

"I'll come down . . ." Cunliffe began.

"No need. No need at all." The doctor quickened his pace towards the head of the stairs. Cunliffe looked too tired to exert himself and Mannering went forward.

"Shall I look up?"

"Oh, if you will— if you will," Cunliffe said gratefully. "Dr. Ignatzi—Mr. Mannering."

Mannering nodded, and Dr. Ignatzi peered at him shortsightedly. There was room for them to walk down the stairs side by side, and as they reached the foot the doctor asked abruptly:

"Are you a friend of the family?"

"An acquaintance."

"I see. Will you be here long?"

"Probably for a few days."

"It would help—I am sure it would be advisable—if Colonel Cunliffe could be persuaded to rest, to take some form of tranquillizer in fact. He is living on his nerves. No doubt you've noticed that."

"I've noticed that he's very edgy, yes."

74

" 'Edgy' is not perhaps a professional description, but it fits the case." They were at the door and Mannering opened it. "Mr. Mannering——"

"Yes?"

"If, in your position of—er—acquaintance and observer, you should deem it advisable that Joanna should be moved at any time, please tell me. My own feeling——" Dr. Ignatzi hesitated, then looked Mannering straight in the eyes, his own enormously magnified by the thick lenses. "My own feeling," he repeated, "is that she would be far better off away from the Manor for a while." They stepped on to the porch. "Forgive my talking in this way, Mr. Mannering, but I am troubled by both father and daughter."

"How long has Joanna's condition worried you?" asked Mannering.

"For nearly a year," answered Dr. Ignatzi. "Now the sister is of a very different temperament; perhaps that is what enabled her to cut the home ties and go and live in London. Mr. Mannering, I beg you to call on me if you think there is the slightest need."

"Certainly I will."

"Very good of you," said Dr. Ignatzi. "Thank you. Goodnight." He nodded jerkily and stepped to his car, drawn up outside the porch.

Mannering waited until he was halfway down the drive, then turned back. He shivered, partly with cold, partly with reaction from the night's events. The act of locking and bolting the door reminded him vividly of Joanna's desperate pleading for those pictures.

Had she really been in such distress for a whole year?

He turned towards the stairs and was halfway up them when Lady Markly appeared from Joanna's room. Her face looked pale and strained.

"How is she?" asked Mannering.

Lady Markly frowned. "I don't know. She's under

75

sedation, of course—all the same, I think I'll sleep in the next-door room just in case she wakes." She paused, her hand on the door handle. Suddenly she swung round.

"Mr. Mannering. I——" She broke off.

"Yes, Lady Markly?" What was she going to tell him, Mannering wondered; from her tone of voice it sounded as if it might be something important.

"It—it doesn't matter."

"If there's anything I can do to help," Mannering began encouragingly. "then please——"

She interrupted him. "No, there's nothing. Nothing at all. Goodnight, Mr. Mannering."

Without another word, she disappeared into the room next to Joanna's, closing the door firmly behind her.

Mannering stirred to bright daylight and a shaft of sunlight striking the wall opposite his bed. For a few moments he lay between sleeping and waking, but gradually the incidents of the previous day formed clear images in his mind. He began, drowsily, to catalogue them.

The man Jenkins, with his story of the old masters at Eliza Doze's cottage and Larraby's statement that Jenkins was an ex-convict. What was the wife's name, the woman left in charge of The Kettle? Doris? No. Nora? No. Ah, *Dora*.

Beverley Willis, with his knowledge of the Cunliffes and his obvious affection for Joanna's sister; Mannering made a mental note that it might be worth talking to Willis, even worth bringing him down to Nether Manor.

The amiable taxi driver with a conscience.

The cottage; frightened Betsy Doze; vicious Harry Anstiss. Mannering could almost see the half-rolled paintings falling from the attic; see Anstiss bound hand and foot; see Joanna, pleading for his release.

Joanna . . .

Joanna, whose motives for wanting the paintings, he had doubted and still had cause to doubt. Joanna, raving like a shrew, trying to frighten him, pleading with him and with her father. Joanna, crouching on the floor with her lovely hair shorn.

Mannering felt the stirring of anger, and reminded himself that it would be easy to take it for granted that Lobb had used those shears.

Joanna, motionless and pale, looking as if she were in a coma.

Cunliffe, putting on a brave act at first, pretending all was well though he was obviously deeply troubled.

Lobb.

Anstiss.

Violet Markly. What had she been going to tell him the previous night, and what had made her change her mind so suddenly?

He remembered her as she had disappeared into the room next to Joanna's; remembered the firm, almost defiant, click of the door.

What was the time now? He lifted his wrist-watch from the bedside table and saw that it was nearly half-past nine. He rang, and within a few minutes a maid arrived with tea.

"Breakfast will be at ten o'clock, sir, but if you would rather have it in your room——?"

"No, thank you," said Mannering, "I'll come down."

The tea was hot and strong; he did not linger over it, and was shaved, bathed and dressed in twenty minutes, and downstairs at five to ten. Middleton, the butler, was hovering discreetly in the breakfast-room.

"Good morning, sir."

"Have the others been down?" asked Mannering.

"The Colonel has, sir. He is now out riding."

"Ah." Mannering sat in the chair Middleton pulled out for him, and was soon tucking into bacon and eggs and coffee as good as anything he had tasted. No one joined him, and twenty minutes later he left the breakfast-room and was walking across the hallway and towards the front door as a red Post Office van sped along the drive; a small man with a remarkably pointed nose delivered both the post and the newspapers—*Times*, *Telegraph* and *Express*. Mannering glanced through the headlines before walking briskly in the direction of the hut to which he had been taken by Lobb and Anstiss the previous night. Today the scene was pleasant and reassuring. The hut door was wide open; close by, a man with a scythe was cutting the long grass, using the instrument with slow, sweeping movements which told of expert knowledge and experience. A long way off, Mannering could see a man on horseback, galloping across parkland.

Hearing someone approaching from behind, he turned, and saw that it was Violet Markly.

"Good morning, Mr. Mannering."

"Good morning. How is Joanna?"

"She hasn't stirred," answered Lady Markly. "Poor child, it was such a shock. Mr. Mannering—what did Dr. Ignatzi say to you last night?"

So she wasn't unobservant, Mannering noted.

"He asked me to give you and your brother any help I could."

"Is that *all?*"

"What else would you expect?" Mannering asked.

"I know he takes a serious view of the anxieties here," said Lady Markly, "and Joanna——"

Mannering interrupted her. "What anxieties?" he asked sharply.

Lady Markly hesitated before replying.

"Joanna—Joanna misses her mother very much," she said at last, "and my brother has never really recovered from the shock of her death. I'm going back to the cottage, Mr. Mannering," she added, with obvious relief at this change of subject. "I've arranged for Betsy Doze to stay with Joanna and to tell me the moment she comes round."

"That's good," Mannering said.

Suddenly, he was anxious to get away from this woman. While she was at the cottage and Cunliffe was out riding there would be ample opportunity to look into the studio again. Returning to the house, he went quickly up the stairs, but the door leading to the north gallery was locked, and it would be showing his hand too obviously to force it. Going to his own room, he found the bed made and everything dusted—and the heavy chair back near the wall, where it belonged. He locked and bolted the door, then reopened the hole in the floor. He listened intently but heard nothing.

But he smelt something—burning.

Burning?

Suddenly tense with alarm, he climbed down the ladder; and now the smell became stronger. There was no sound, no feeling of a hostile presence to warn him, only the thickening air. Nearing the door to the studio he opened it slowly, cautiously, aware of the danger of a sudden draught, horribly alive to the terrible memory of the burning cottage.

Over in the far corner, near the paint store, the canvases and the hardboard, a pile of rags was smouldering, a little patch of flame dancing about them. Near the rags was a plastic bag which looked as if it were filled with water.

Water? Mannering realized in a flash that it could be petrol. If it were, and if it exploded, then the whole place would be alight.

CHAPTER TEN

THE DANGER

The innocent-looking plastic bag was twenty feet away from Mannering, but within inches of the smouldering rags. If the flames leapt suddenly they might well touch it.

He remembered the explosive sounds in the cottage—just such sounds as would be made if this bag did burst and it did contain petrol.

As these thoughts were sweeping through his mind he was moving swiftly but steadily towards the bench. A flame leapt two inches into the air. It was very hot. He could see only the liquid in the plastic bag, liquid which he now noted was slightly yellowed, lacking the clarity of clear water. Lifting a piece of hardboard with agonising slowness—any quick displacement of air might well fan the flames in the wrong direction—he placed it firmly between the rags and the plastic bag, and wedged it in position.

His mouth was very dry.

With another piece of hardboard he pushed the rags further away, close to the edge of the bench. Then he placed the board on top of them; that should smother the flames. The smell of burning was nauseatingly unpleasant.

Keeping a hand in front of his face, he watched the plastic bag. Overheated by the flames, it might well explode at a touch; and though, with every moment, the risk of an explosion was lessening, he would be wise not to handle it for some time. He began to look about him and saw another, similar, bag in the corner where, on his last visit to the studio, he had seen the copy of the Franz Hals portrait.

The portrait wasn't there.

The second bag was quite cool and he picked it up. This, too, was made of plastic, with a rubber band round the neck, rather like a toy balloon. He loosened this band carefully, smelling, as he did so, the faint but unmistakable fumes of petrol.

He looked across at the other bag, beginning to take in the situation in more detail. Once the fire had taken a hold, this studio would have been wrecked, and so would the gallery above it. Even if the rest of the house had been saved, the whole of the north side of the Manor would have been burned out.

Who would take such a risk, and—*why?*

Why had Anstiss set fire to the attic at the cottage?

Obviously, thought Mannering, to destroy something that he and Lobb were anxious that no one should discover; so, presumably, the same kind of "something" was here in the studio. His heart began to beat faster. Search, and he would find.

Just as he had taken it for granted that Lobb had cut off Joanna's hair, so, now, he was taking it for granted that Anstiss had started this fire. It wasn't absolutely certain, but it was highly probable.

Why?

What was there here which had to be destroyed?

What had there been in the attic at the cottage?

He began to search, looking behind every picture, on every shelf, moving everything so that he could be sure he overlooked nothing. Gradually he became absorbed in the task, so much so that he lost all count of time—all thought of danger, too.

Suddenly he heard a sound from the top of the spiral staircase, and realized that someone was approaching the stairs from the gallery.

He moved back cautiously, stepping behind an easel supporting a large canvas.

The door leading from the gallery to the stairs opened, and a pair of highly polished riding-boots appeared, then a man's legs, then the skirt of his jacket.

It was Colonel Cunliffe.

Cunliffe left the door open and clumped down the stairs quite briskly. He sniffed, looking about the studio without appearing to notice Mannering. The plastic bag, however, caught his eye, and he went straight over to it. His hand hovered; Mannering was tempted to shout: "Don't touch it," but it was probably cool enough to be handled by now. Cunliffe was cautious, after all, and merely lifted the hardboard off the rags. Smoke billowed up, sending him back, gasping.

"What the devil!" he exclaimed.

He stood staring at the rags, wrinkling his nose. Then he turned and stared at the paintings, running his hand over the back of his head. "Can't understand it," he muttered. "Who would want to burn the place down?"

Now he leaned over the plastic bag, sniffed, then backed away. Slowly he buried his face in his hands; at that moment he was remarkably like his daughter, giving the same impression of helplessness and hopelessness that she had given when crouched in grief at the foot of the stairs.

"Will it *never* end?" he asked, despairingly. "Will it *never* end?"

Presently he straightened up, and brushing the rags on to the hardboard, he carried them to the sink and ran water over the now all but dead embers. He stared at the tap as the water sprayed out, then washed and dried his hands with unthinking thoroughness. Mannering could see him very clearly, could not mistake the look of despair on his features.

"Joanna," he said sadly. "Oh, Joanna."

He looked about the shelves and seemed to be making sure that there were no other smouldering rags. Then he turned and stared at the painted trifles.

"Joanna," he repeated.

At last he went up the stairs, his step that of an old and weary man. The gallery door closed. Cautiously Mannering moved from his hiding-place, the picture of Cunliffe's despair vivid in his mind's eye as he continued his search.

He found nothing that could have the least significance.

He went round once again and then stood where Cunliffe had stood, in front of the gay little modern paintings. For the first time he saw the initials J.C. in the bottom left-hand corner of each. These were the only finished paintings, the only things of any conceivable value here, and no one could possibly believe they were worth more than a few pounds, unless . . .

He took one off the wall and carried it to the clear north light beneath the window. Any art student with the slightest flair could do as well or better. Fetching a small bottle of methylated spirits and a piece of clean rag, he dampened a spot on the rag and carefully rubbed a corner of the painting. The pale blue of the sky came off on to the rag almost immediately. He dampened another spot, and worked on the same corner again with even greater care.

He did not get down to the canvas, for there was darker paint beneath the blue. He cleaned a slightly larger area and found traces of varnish, reddish-brown colour and a small speck of bright yellow, strangely reminiscent of the Franz Hals portrait he had seen on his earlier visit. He stopped, putting canvas and rag down, and studied the picture.

Why had Joanna painted her trifles over an old canvas? And why should the incendiary want to destroy them?

Mannering drew back from the painting, picked up the palette, worked some pale blue on to a brush and painted over the corner which he had cleaned. Now he had to make up his mind whether to leave the paintings here or take them away. There was an obvious risk of another attack, and the perfect answer would be to watch both entrances. It wasn't possible by himself.

Whoever wanted to destroy the paintings certainly didn't want them found and would be alarmed if they disappeared. But it was possible that one wouldn't be missed—or even two.

The decision made, Mannering picked up the canvas he had just been working on, selected one other, also signed with the initials J.C., and tucked them under his arm. As he went awkwardly up the ladder he moved carefully and warily, alive to the danger that someone might have discovered that he was missing.

His room, however, was exactly as he had left it.

He slipped the paintings under his mattress, and went out, leaving his door unlocked. A maid was coming out of Joanna's room.

"How is Miss Joanna?"

"About the same, sir."

"So she's no better," said Mannering heavily. "Who's with her?"

"Betsy Doze, sir."

Mannering nodded, gave a perfunctory tap at the door and went in. Betsy, on a chair near the bed, was knitting and looking at a magazine at the same time. She jumped up, clutching at the falling ball of wool.

"Good—good morning, sir!"

"Hallo, Betsy," Mannering said. "I've just come to see Miss Joanna."

He looked down—and was shocked.

Joanna had been tucked tightly into bed so that only her head and face showed, a scarf twisted in a nun-like coif about her head. She lay, still as death, and very pale. Mannering frowned, studying her lips for some sign of movement. He touched the lid of her right eye, raised it for a moment, then gently lowered it again.

"She—she looks pretty bad, doesn't she?" Betsy asked uneasily.

"She'll get over it," Mannering assured her, but he did not feel anything like as confident as he sounded. "Look after her." He went out, striding back to his own room, knowing exactly what he wanted to do. Seizing the telephone beside his bed, he dialled Dr. Ignatzi's number.

A pleasant-voiced woman answered him. "I'm afraid the doctor is out, who . . . ? Oh, yes, he *did* leave a number, Mr. Mannering . . . Yes, I'll call him . . . To come to the Manor urgently . . . Can I give him any idea what to expect?"

Mannering, knowing that someone might be listening in, said: "I think Joanna may have taken an overdose of some sleeping mixture, probably one with morphia in it."

"I'll see that my husband is told right away."

"Thank you," said Mannering. "Thank you very much. It really *is* urgent."

He rang off, wondering whether he would have been wiser to send for an ambulance and get the girl to a hospital without delay; but she was breathing evenly enough, and Ignatzi surely wouldn't be long. Even so, Mannering knew that he would be on edge for the next half hour or so; he must find something to occupy his mind until Ignatzi arrived.

Walking round to the back of the house, he found a groom brushing down Joanna's chestnut in a stable yard close by the garage.

"Do you know where I'll find Miss Hester's car?" he

85

asked. "Colonel Cunliffe was good enough to say I could use it."

"The red Mini, sir—it's in the end garage, Number Six, and the key will be in the ignition. We always leave the key in during the day in case someone needs it in a hurry."

Mannering drove round to the front of the house; the car was comfortable enough and had good leg room. He parked it in the shade of a big lime tree. It was warm; this was as good a spell of weather as England had had all the summer.

A little low-on-the-ground Triumph was coming rapidly up the drive, and Mannering was surprised and relieved to see Ignatzi climb out of it. He was wearing ginger-colored tweeds and golfing shoes; there wasn't much doubt about where he'd been. Seeing Mannering, he half turned, but Mannering shook his head and Ignatzi took the hint and went straight into the house. Mannering strolled about the ornamental garden, half his mind admiring the roses, the dahlias, the early chrysanthemums, the other half pre-occupied with Joanna.

Ignatzi was taking his time; he must have been there at least half an hour, Mannering thought. Then he heard another engine, and saw a white ambulance coming along the drive.

So he's worried too, Mannering thought grimly.

He did not wait to see Joanna brought out of the Manor, but got back into Hester Cunliffe's car and drove out of the grounds towards the village. The blackened ruin of Eliza Doze's cottage showed clearly, as he rounded a bend in the road.

Had there been disguised paintings there, as well?

It was difficult to associate the thatched cottages and the atmosphere of peacefulness with fire and violence and the threat of death; difficult to realise that, until last evening, he had never seen this place. Pulling up by the telephone kiosk outside the village store, he stepped inside and put in a call to Quinns. Larraby was on the line, almost immediately. "Find out what you can about a man named Harry Anstiss, obviously a practiced thief," Mannering told him, "and another named Lobb, a big, powerfully built man who can paint. Ring me back at the Manor. If you can find out nothing, say so. If either has a record just say the answer is in the affirmative. All clear, Josh?"

"Quite clear, sir."

Mannering rang off, and immediately dialed Dr. Ignatzi's number; the same woman answered him.

"Sorry to worry you again," Mannering said.

"Oh, that's all right, Mr. Mannering."

"I'd like to call in and see Dr. Ignatzi when he's had a chance to examine Joanna Cunliffe," Mannering said. "What would be a good time?"

"Well—would six o'clock be too late?"

"Six o'clock will be fine. Thank you."

Leaving the kiosk, he went into the village shop, small, but surprisingly bright, the shelves stacked with fresh-looking tins and packets. He bought some cigarettes from a middle-aged woman who was pleasant enough, but uncommunicative. He had a feeling that she knew who he was and was determined in advance not to be drawn. As he drove slowly, thoughtfully, back to the Manor, first Ignatzi in his Triumph and then the ambulance passed him. He saw one or two men working in the ornamental garden, others on the lawns.

"He must keep a staff of twenty," Mannering reflected.

Leaving the car outside the front door, he went into the house. It was past two o'clock, so he had missed luncheon, but after his late breakfast this was something he could well do without. Going straight to his room, he lifted the mattress to make sure that the paintings he had taken from the studio were still there. They were.

Suddenly there was a tap at the door. Swiftly he lowered the mattress and smoothed the coverlet.

"Come in," he called.

After a short pause, Cunliffe entered. He looked tired and very much older, and his shoulders sagged dejectedly.

"They've taken Joanna to the hospital," he announced. "Ignatzi seems worried about her." He lifted his hands and let them fall. "And I, too, am deeply worried. Mannering, forgive me if, once again, I take advantage of your presence here, but I would very much appreciate some—some guidance from you, both on a matter of business which affects us both and on a personal matter. Have you time to listen?"

"And to help, if I can," promised Mannering.

CHAPTER ELEVEN

COLONEL CUNLIFFE CONFIDES

"I've been very worried about Joanna for over a year," said Cunliffe. He had taken Mannering to his upstairs library, a room of elegance and glowing beauty. Half of one wall was covered with miniatures, possibly by Nicholas Hilliard, and Mannering's expert eye told him that this collection alone would fetch at least a hundred thousand pounds at any big auction. There was a Gainsborough portrait too, and on one narrow wall a magnificent painting of Nether Manor, almost certainly by Constable. "My sister put it down to the fact that she lost her mother at an impressionable age," Cunliffe went on, "yet I am a long way from being sure that is the right explanation. I believe——"

He hesitated, and squared his shoulders as if to make a supreme effort.

"What do you believe?" asked Mannering sharply.

Cunliffe drew a deep breath. "I have reason to suspect that it is Joanna who has taken the paintings and replaced them by copies. I do not, I cannot, believe that she would do such things for personal gain, and so it follows that she must be—she must be ill. Mannering"—Cunliffe paused and there was a film of tears in his eyes—"these paintings mean so much to me, as I told you. Two days ago I would never have believed that Joanna would touch them, whatever the circumstances. Now, I am not so sure."

"But that hideous attack on her," Mannering said slowly.

"Surely——"

"People who are mentally—mentally unbalanced"—Cunliffe got the words out with an effort—"do strange things, Mannering. I'm very much afraid that Joanna may herself have——" He broke off, glancing at a grandfather clock in a corner of the room. "I should soon have a message from the hospital; Ignatzi promised to call the moment the specialist had seen her. Did you know that she was an amateur painter?" he added abruptly.

Mannering had no wish to disclose, even to his host, his knowledge of the studio beneath the north gallery. "No, I didn't," he said easily.

"She spent a year at the Slade, and although she isn't particularly good, she paints quite pleasantly. Some years ago my wife used to clean and frame the paintings here —it was her hobby and she was better than many professionals. Since she died, the workshop—beneath the north gallery—has been used as a studio by Joanna. I went down there this morning, to search for some clue as to her behavior, her distress—and do you know what I found?" He did not wait for an answer but went on unbelievingly: "I found smouldering rags and—and a plastic bag filled with petrol! Petrol! Mannering, if that had ignited, the whole house might have been burned down!"

"Petrol!" exclaimed Mannering, in assumed astonishment. "But Joanna couldn't . . ."

"I don't know, Mannering. I simply don't know. But I *do* know that no week, hardly a day, passes now without some fresh cause for anxiety. Mannering—there is a barrier between Joanna and me. There was a time when she would confide in me, but now she keeps everything to herself."

"Don't you think a doctor, even a psychiatrist . . . ?" Mannering asked.

Cunliffe's manner changed. His eyes flashed, and he sat erect in his chair, his hands clenched.

"Psychiatrist? What the devil do you mean? Do you think my daughter is *mad?*"

"That's the last thing I meant," Mannering said soothingly. "It's just that psychiatrists are experts in gaining a patient's confidence." He paused for a moment, before asking suddenly: "Why do you allow a man like Lobb on the premises?"

He brought the name out casually and without the slightest warning, remembering the effect it had had on Joanna. But Cunliffe only frowned.

"I know of no one named Lobb."

"What about Anstiss?"

"The second footman?"

"Yes."

"He is a very good servant. My daughter——"

"He is a thief," Mannering said quietly.

"Anstiss—a *thief?*"

"An art thief."

"Good God!" exclaimed Cunliffe. "You really mean ——" He sank back in his chair. "But Joanna recommended him! She said he had worked for years for the family of a friend of hers, who were cutting down on the staff. A—*thief?*"

"I think you'll find that he has a record."

"It's—it's unbelievable. Joanna couldn't have known. She——" Cunliffe broke off again, as if he had suddenly realized that in the circumstances it would not be surprising if his daughter had indeed known the truth about Anstiss. Very slowly he got up, and moved towards the window overlooking the ornamental garden. Two cedars

91

of Lebanon stood out against a copse of green and copper beech.

"I'll be in my room——" Mannering began.

"Please don't go," Cunliffe said. After a long pause, he went on: "Will you come and join me, Mannering?" His voice had changed and become much softer. As Mannering reached his side he waved his hand towards the view, with its beauty, its colour, its grandeur. "Mannering," he went on, "Cunliffes have owned this land for generations. Cunliffes have ridden out from Nether Manor for a hundred selfless missions. Five men from our family died in the Crusades, two at Crecy and four at Agincourt. My father drove away from here for the First World War, and didn't return. I left here for the Second World War, more fortunate than he, for I came home. There is"—he gestured again, this time to the leather-bound tomes on one wall, larger books than most—"there is the written history of the family—illustrated works begun by monks who helped to build Salisbury Cathedral. Much Cunliffe money was spent in the cathedral; much of the wood for pews and choir-stalls, beams and reredos, was from trees felled in these grounds. You"—Cunliffe paused, then turned slowly to face Mannering—"you are a man who can understand what such things as these mean; what a source of pride they are."

"I can indeed," Mannering told him.

"A source of pride," Cunliffe repeated in a far-away voice. "Mannering, if you were to read those books, the history of this family, you would find the truth in them. There have been dishonourable members of the family. One was hanged, for treason, another burned at the stake for heresy. Some have been judged mad."

This time Mannering did not speak.

"Yes," said Cunliffe, huskily. "There has always been a streak of madness in the family." His lips twisted. "You will better understand why I was so sensitive just now." Mannering nodded but did not interrupt. "I have this

92

grave anxiety about Joanna, whom I so dearly love. If I am right and she is—is double-dealing, is it because she is unbalanced? Or is it because she has inherited those qualities which can bring dishonor?"

Mannering looked grave. "I don't know," he said slowly.

"The possibility of either torments me." Cunliffe passed a hand wearily across his forehead. "I am the last surviving member of the male line. All that I have, all that the family has, will go to my eldest grandson, should I be fortunate enough to have one. But neither of my daughters is yet married, and I may well be the last Cunliffe to own Nether Manor. I cannot go to the police about those missing pictures, Mannering. Nor can I ask a psychiatrist to examine my daughter. If the police were to discover a criminal streak, or the doctors to find evidence of mental instability in any one of the family——"

He paused, as if at a loss for words, and in that instant the telephone bell rang. Cunliffe did not move to answer it at first; then, as if awakened from a trance, he snatched up the receiver.

"Colonel Cunliffe." To Mannering, he mouthed: "*It might be about Joanna.*" Tense and still, he stood beside his desk. "Yes, yes . . . oh, is there any—any immediate danger?" Anxiety leapt expressively to his mouth, his eyes. "There isn't . . . Thank you, thank you for calling."

He rang off, moistening his lips, and turned to Mannering.

"They are going to keep her at the Infirmary, under observation."

"The best thing that could happen," Mannering said reassuringly. "What she needs is a complete rest."

While touched by Colonel Cunliffe's obvious distress, he could not bring himself to believe that Joanna was in fact mentally unbalanced. Far more likely, he thought, that, as he had originally suspected, the girl was being blackmailed. As Colonel Cunliffe had himself said, so many strange things had happened, and Joanna could hardly be responsible for them all.

No, something very sinister was going on in the village of Nether Wylie, and while anxious not to abuse his host's hospitality, Mannering knew he would be unable to rest until he had discovered exactly what it was.

Half an hour later, he was back in his own room. Nothing had been touched; it was possible that no one had yet noticed that Joanna's pictures had been taken from the studio. But as he lifted them from beneath the mattress, the telephone bell rang—he never seemed to be able to touch them without some interruption, Mannering thought resignedly, as he reached for the receiver.

"A call for you from London, sir," a girl said. The next moment Josh Larraby was on the line.

"Mr. Mannering?"

"Yes, Josh." Mannering felt excitement stirring.

"So far as the first is concerned, the answer is in the affirmative," Larraby said. So Anstiss *did* have a police record. "I can discover nothing about the other matter."

"Keep trying," urged Mannering. "It's even more important."

He rang off, picked up the pictures and carried them under his arm down to the car. It was now after four o'clock and he wanted to go into Salisbury and visit The Kettle before seeing Dr. Ignatzi. Before starting off, he told Middleton that he would be back soon after eight o'clock. The afternoon was warm and pleasant, and the little car hummed smoothly; he had so much on his mind that it was a good thing the car almost drove itself.

He went through the gateway leading on to the main road, taking his time. He saw a lorry coming from Salisbury, but there was plenty of room to turn towards the city and it did not occur to him to wait.

As he reached the road, the lorry swung towards him. One moment he was completely free from fear; the next, terror leapt to his heart, to his throat. The front of the huge vehicle towered crushingly above him; if it struck it would demolish the little car and hurl him to death.

He swung the wheel to the left, in desperation.

He saw the lorry loom up like a monster, but its front wheels passed him; he still had a chance.

Then the lorry caught the back of the Mini and spun it round in wild gyrations. A door flew open and he was flung on to the thick grass of the verge. Pieces of the car flew past him; something smacked into the ground only inches from his head.

The roar of the lorry's engine, menacing, inexorable, screamed a warning to his ear.

CHAPTER TWELVE

THREAT OF DEATH

The shock of realisation made Mannering sharply, fearfully, alert. He lay on his side, body quivering, facing the road, and now he could see the lorry coming towards him, could even make out the head and shoulders of the driver although he could not discern the features. He drew in his breath and straightened his arms and legs; there was only one hope, that he could roll out of the way of the oncoming wheels. Subconsciously, he realized that if he began to move too soon, the driver could change direction, and, teeth gritted, he waited for the wheels to mount the verge.

Then he rolled towards the right.

Once again he heard the roar of the engine, the scream of the merciless wheels as they skidded on the damp grass, then felt himself sliding downwards, out of control; he was in a ditch. He thudded to the bottom and lay spread-eagled on his back, seeing leaves and the branches of trees vivid against the sky. He grew tense, fearful that the machine of death would loom over the edge and come rushing down. The shadow of one gigantic wheel touched him. He half turned again, but there was nothing he could do, no way he could escape.

The shadow disappeared. The engine snarling a re-treat.

He lay still, becoming as one with his surroundings, as a wild animal attempts to foil pursuit. Suddenly, a man appeared at the top of the ditch, in a strangely fore-shortened view, his face shadowed and round, his glasses like lamps.

"Here he is!" he called.

A woman appeared by his side, hair frizzed to a ginger halo.

"Is he hurt?"

"His eyes are open."

"There's blood on his forehead."

"Go and stop the next car," the man urged. "I'll get down to him."

The woman disappeared, and the man put one foot cautiously over the edge, arms stretched out to balance himself.

"Are you all right?" he asked anxiously.

Mannering muttered an incoherent answer.

"Don't move!" The man was level with him now. "I know a bit about first aid, let's see if there're any bones broken." He ran his hands up and down Mannering's arms and legs and then about his back and chest. "Doesn't seem to be any trouble. Think you can get up? Let me give you a hand—watch it now, easy does it."

Mannering, grunting, stumbled to his feet. He was dizzy, and swayed to one side; the man grabbed him.

"Take your time, then. No hurry."

"You—you're very good."

"Oh, nonsense. *Can* you manage? Someone else will soon be along."

"I'll be okay." Except that his left shoulder hurt, Man-nering could manage well enough. Supported by his res-cuer, he reached the top of the ditch.

Fifty yards away, on its roof and with the rear crushed

in and the windscreen and windows shattered, lay the red Mini. Nearer, parked off the road, was a white Rover. Legs firmly planted, the ginger-haired woman was waving down an approaching car. It slowed. Mannering felt a trickle on his right eye and wiped it with the back of his hand; blood dripped from his fingers.

He swayed again.

He heard the man say: "Quicker we get you to hospital the better."

Voices and figures surrounded him. But there was no sign of the lorry except the marks of its wheels where it had scarred the soft ground, and where it could so easily have killed him.

"There you are, sir. Is that easier?" A Jamaican nurse stood back and examined the patch of plaster on Mannering's forehead.

"Much easier," Mannering said gratefully.

"And your shoulder?"

"Tender but movable," answered Mannering.

"You were very lucky to get away with it as well as you did, sir."

"Believe me, I know it," Mannering said with feeling.

He walked out of the casualty ward at the Salisbury Infirmary, smiled on by the nurse and by an elderly woman coming towards the ward. Stepping into the small courtyard where cars and an ambulance were parked, he saw a police car in one corner, two policemen sitting at the front. The one in the driving seat got out and approached him.

"Mr. Mannering?"

"Yes."

"I'm Police Sergeant Webster, sir. I'd be very grateful if you'd come up to the station for a few minutes."

"What time is it?" asked Mannering.

"Half-past five, sir."

"I'm due to see Dr. Ignatzi at six o'clock, and I'd like to look in at a shop called The Kettle on the way."

"The shop will be closed," the sergeant said. "We'll see you're in good time for your appointment with Dr. Ignatzi."

"In that case——" Mannering shrugged.

The police station, new and bare-looking, stood well back from a main road. The sergeant drove him to the front entrance, and the other man took him inside to an office more like a hospital than the hospital from which Mannering had just come. A big, raw-boned man in uniform, with an inspector's stars on his shoulders, was sitting at a desk.

"Mr. Mannering," said the policeman.

"Oh, yes." The other man stood up. "I'm Chief Inspector Fishlock, Mr. Mannering." He shook hands, while looking searchingly at the plaster on Mannering's forehead. "Please sit down." The door closed on the policeman. "You seem to have been very lucky, sir."

"Meaning, I ought to be dead."

"You might well have been."

"Yes. I know."

"Mr. and Mrs. Anderson, of Gloucester, saw your car by the side of the road, and stopped," Fishlock told him. "They made a statement after seeing you to the Infirmary."

"Do you have their address? I'd like to thank them."

"I'll see you get it, sir. They reported seeing a lorry driving in the vicinity of the accident at what they described as a 'crazy speed.' Were you struck by a lorry?"

Mannering hesitated.

Fishlock had very clear, very direct, grey eyes, and good, weathered features. He kept remarkably still as he talked, only his lips moving. The pause lengthened but he did not prompt Mannering, who finally made up his mind that there was a limit to what he could withhold from the police.

"Yes," he said. "It was attempted murder."

Fishlock showed no change of expression. "In your opinion, a deliberate attempt to run you down?" he asked.

"Yes."

"Did you see the driver?"

"Not well enough to distinguish his features."

"I see, sir. What makes you think it was deliberate, and that it wasn't simply a case of the driver losing control?"

"A vehicle out of control is obviously out of control," Mannering said. "The marks on the grass are a clear indication that this one was not. There is also the fact that the driver didn't stop."

"I see." Fishlock was over-formal. "We've been to the scene of the incident, sir, and taken measurements and photographs."

"Did you examine my car?"

"The Mini, you mean? Yes, sir."

"There were two pictures in it," Mannering said. "I was taking them to a dealer."

"No pictures were found, sir."

"Have you found the lorry?" asked Mannering.

"Yes. It had been stolen from a quarry, a few miles along the road."

"The driver?"

Chief Inspector Fishlock frowned. "No trace of him, sir, and no fingerprints on the steering wheel. Why should anyone wish to run you down?" he added. When Mannering didn't answer, he went on: "Could it be anything to do with these, sir?" He leaned back and took a package from the wall behind him—a package containing seven canvases, each flattened out, each with paper over the painted surface. He removed the paper from the top canvas and placed it on his desk.

It appeared to be identical with the Vermeer which hung in the north gallery at Nether Manor. Mannering studied it without expression, and then asked:

"Is this one of the paintings I sent here with the taxi driver?"

"Don't you *know*, sir?" Fishlock allowed himself to sound sceptical.

Mannering flashed a smile.

"No, Inspector."

"But *you* gave them to the taxi driver!"

"Yes, I did. Do you want to hear the whole story?" Mannering asked.

"In the form of a statement, sir?"

"If you want to have it taken down, I don't mind," Mannering assured him.

"Would you object if the statement were taped?"

"It might be a very good idea," Mannering said.

Fishlock lifted a tape-recorder from his desk, plugged it into a point behind him and then switched on. The spools began to turn at once.

Mannering said clearly: "Yesterday morning I received a letter from a Mrs. Eliza Doze stating that she thought some pictures in her attic might be valuable, but that she did not want to tell local dealers. Such finds are rare. I thought it worth coming to see for myself, particularly as knowledge of them had also reached a local dealer."

Fishlock nodded.

"Before I reached Mrs. Doze she had been attacked and taken to hospital. I went into her cottage to look for the pictures and found a man in the attic. He had those." Mannering pointed. "I took them from him and put him in my taxi, but there was a lot of excitement because the cottage suddenly went up in flames, and he got away. I sent the paintings here, for safe keeping, and spent the night at Nether Manor."

"Were you going there, sir, in any case?"

"No. Miss Joanna Cunliffe invited me when she realised that I had nowhere to stay. And I was so intrigued by what had happened that I preferred to stay in the neighborhood."

"And while you were at the Manor, the young lady herself was attacked," Fishlock said.

"Yes."

"Did you see the assault, sir?"

"I saw her immediately after it; her screams roused the entire household, but I didn't see who attacked her. I inquired at the hospital and was told she was still under sedation."

"So I understand, sir. Why didn't you tell us the truth about the paintings last night?"

"Seemed a little too involved to explain over the telephone. They were in your possession and could hardly be safer. I would have come to see you. In fact," added Mannering, "I was on the way when attacked by the lorry."

"Which leads me to a question I asked earlier, sir. Why do you think the attack was made on you?"

Mannering shrugged. "I can't tell you what I don't know."

"No, sir, not if you don't know." Fishlock allowed doubt to hang in the air. "But have you told us everything you do know? Did you, for instance, come here solely to see Eliza Doze?"

"Yes, Inspector, I did."

"You hadn't been invited by anyone else?"

"No, only by Mrs. Doze." Mannering looked at his watch. "I've an appointment with Dr. Ignatzi at six o'clock, Inspector—it's ten to six now, isn't it?"

"Yes, sir." Chief Inspector Fishlock hesitated, then leaned back. "I understand you also wanted to see the owner of The Kettle, an antique shop here."

"Yes. He was the local dealer I mentioned."

"Do you know how he came to hear about the paintings at the cottage?"

"I've no idea. I'd hoped to find out."

"Mr. Mannering," said Chief Inspector Fishlock, "we're not unaware of your reputation and of the fact that the Metropolitan Police have often been grateful for your help. We know that in your particular business you have to be very discreet, but may we rely on you to tell us anything—*anything*," repeated Fishlock emphatically, "you feel we ought to know?"

"Anything I feel you ought to know," murmured Mannering. "You certainly may, Inspector," he added blandly.

"Thank you, sir."

"Will you hold those paintings and tell no one about them?"

Fishlock gave a faint smile.

"You can rely on us too, sir."

"Thank *you*," said Mannering. "Did you know that Jenkins of The Kettle had a police record?"

"Yes," Fishlock answered flatly. He pressed a bell, and almost at once the door opened and the policeman appeared.

"Take Mr. Mannering to Dr. Ignatzi's house, will you?"

"Yes, sir."

Five minutes later, Mannering was sitting next to the driver as they drove along streets of houses and shops, some old, some new, then past the cathedral, its stately spire austerely rising against a foregound of trees and sweeping lawns. Within the Cathedral Close the world of bustle and business and crime seemed to fade away; there was a hush, even a sense of sanctity, in the beauty of the Georgian and Elizabethan houses which flanked it.

Dr. Ignatzi lived in a house the front of which overlooked the cathedral. The door was opened by a plump, bright-eyed woman who obviously recognized Mannering; she noted his injured forehead, but made no comment.

"Good evening, Mr. Mannering. My husband is back. Please come in."

She led the way to a room at the front of the house. Ignatzi was standing by the window looking at the cathedral through a bower of bush roses. He looked pale and tired.

"Good evening, Mr. Mannering . . . What will you have? . . . A whisky and soda with that head? . . . I'd settle for sherry, if I were you . . ." He talked briskly, conversationally, until they were both seated in chintz-covered armchairs; then Dr. Ignatzi lowered his glass sharply. "When you sent for me, did you realise that Joanna Cunliffe had been given morphia?"

"Yes. The pinpoint pupils gave that away."

"It was a good job you discovered it," Ignatzi said. "If she'd been much later at the hospital, she might have been very ill indeed. She took morphia by mouth, Mannering. Either she recovered well enough to try to commit suicide, or an attempt was made to murder her. Had you realized *that?*"

CHAPTER THIRTEEN

ATTEMPTED MURDER?

Mannering stood up and moved towards the window, looking out at the cathedral spire. It seemed wrong to be talking of violence and of murder here. A group of children were walking diagonally across the lawns, passing beneath a cedar of Lebanon whose branches swept the ground.

"I know she is in deep trouble," he said at last.

"That doesn't answer my question," said Ignatzi.

"No. You saw her last night." Mannering turned to face the doctor. "You gave her an injection. Could she have come round from that in time to dose herself with morphia?"

"I wouldn't have thought so."

"Have you told the police?" Mannering demanded.

"They will be told by the hospital authorities."

"And when you're questioned will you state that you think it might have been attempted murder?"

"I think I shall have to," Ignatzi said uneasily. He placed a hand on the high dome of his forehead, looking troubled. "I know the family well, I don't want to make the situation worse than it is, but—yes. I shall have to make it clear that I think she was given the tablets and that it was—may have been—attempted murder."

"The police already know there was an attempt to murder me," said Mannering.

Ignatzi stopped his glass halfway to his lips.

"How was that?"

"I was run down by a lorry. Dr. Ignatzi, how long have you known there was trouble in the Cunliffe family?"

"For the better part of a year."

"Have you any idea what it's about?"

"None at all." Ignatzi sipped his drink. "Lady Markly put it down to the delayed effect on the Colonel and Joanna of the death of the Colonel's wife. I don't think that's true. Certainly Cunliffe had a bad year after her death, but——"

"Did you attend her?" interrupted Mannering.

"Yes. I have been the family doctor since I took over this practice just after the end of the war. Cunliffe was almost inconsolable—they had been so very close—but Joanna was away at school at the time. I saw her at the funeral and on holiday from time to time, and I would have said that her reaction was normal for a child of her age. Certainly nothing would lead me to expect that she had buried her grief for five years and then had this kind of reaction to it. Whatever the cause of the trouble I think it's comparatively recent."

"Is there any history of insanity in the family?"

Ignatzi looked startled.

"What makes you ask that?"

"It's an old family," Mannering said evasively. "Sometimes if there's too much inbreeding——"

"There's a rumor of a brother, or maybe cousin, who spent much of his life in a private sanatorium," Ignatzi said slowly. "And I've heard other rumors, but I've seen absolutely no sign of mental instability in any member of this family, no sign at all. Whatever the cause of this trouble," he added with an air of finality, "I am convinced it comes from a situation, not from a mental condition."

"What kind of situation?"

Ignatzi frowned. "Joanna has been frightened."

"Could it be due to blackmail?"

"Obviously it could, although I can't imagine anything in her life bad enough for blackmail. Mannering, you say there was an attempt to run you down?"

"Yes."

"But why?"

"Possibly because someone's afraid I might find out what's happening at the Manor," Mannering answered.

Ignatzi put his glass down on a round, glass-topped table.

"You are *that* Mannering, then? I'd never heard of you, but my wife seems to think you're some kind of wizard." He gave a little, embarrassed laugh. "Forgive my clumsy way of putting it. She has read about you in the newspapers from time to time. Would—er—would you mind if she joins us?"

"Of course not," Mannering said.

"She may ask you a great number of questions."

"I'll answer them if I can," promised Mannering. "But before she comes I'd like to confirm one or two things." He moved back to his chair. "Both Joanna and her father have been behaving a little oddly for a year. Joanna's badly frightened by something but you don't know what. Her sister——"

"I don't often see Hester," interrupted Ignatzi. "She left the Manor three or four years ago. Being five years older than Joanna, everyone assumed she would take her mother's place as hostess, but she went to live in London."

"Lady Markly?" asked Mannering.

"She won't live at the Manor, preferring life in her cottage," said Ignatzi. "She acts as hostess on formal occasions, but the Cunliffes don't do very much entertaining these days. At one time the Manor seethed with activity. A pity they gave it up." Ignatzi paused, and then asked: "Have you come to Salisbury for any particular reason?"

"I came to see an Eliza Doze, who wanted me to have a look at some paintings."

"Now *there's* a character!" exclaimed Ignatzi. "I saw her only this afternoon. She's in a public ward of the Infirmary, but ready to get up and go after her assailants any moment."

"Can I see her?"

"This evening?"

"Preferably," said Mannering. "But in a private ward."

"I'll see what I can arrange," promised Ignatzi. He went to the door and disappeared for a moment, then came back with his wife, who preceded him with some eagerness.

"I knew you were *the* John Mannering," she said warmly. "I've seen your picture in the papers too often to have any doubt. Do tell me—is there some great crime being staged at the Manor?"

"Don't answer!" cried Ignatzi, with pretended merriment. "Even if there is a crime in preparation, don't answer. I should be hearing about it for the next two months. I'll telephone the hospital." He hurried out, watched by his wife, and Mannering saw the brightness fade from her eyes, to be replaced by a very sober look indeed.

"My husband is worried by what is happening at the Manor," she said. "There is a lot he won't tell me because of professional etiquette, but sometimes I have thought he was frightened, as well as Joanna. If you can do anything to solve the problem, Mr. Mannering, you will be doing a very great service indeed."

Ten minutes later, Mannering left Dr. Ignatzi's house and made his way to the nearest garage. The Mini would take several weeks to repair, and it would be impossible to continue his investigations on foot, or, he thought drily, by courtesy of the police. Country-town garages were not always able or willing to hire out a car at short notice, but in this he was lucky. The owner, working overtime, proved both civil and efficient, and in less than half an hour Mannering was heading for the hospital and Eliza Doze, at the steering wheel of a sleek, inconspicuously gray, Ford Cortina.

A youth on duty was expecting him, and gave him directions to the private wards. There he was met by a small, middle-aged woman, the Night Sister.

"It's a great pleasure to meet you, Mr. Mannering . . . And although she may not admit it, Eliza Doze is very proud that you've come to see her." She led the way along a passage into a room overlooking a tennis court and some old buildings.

Eliza Doze was sitting up in bed in a small, austerely furnished ward. She looked very old and brown and wizened against the brightness of her deep-set eyes. Her fine, thin mouth, her nose, large, hooked, and well-cut, lent a certain air of authenticity to an almost regal manner.

"Eliza, I have brought Mr. Mannering to see you."

"Good evening, Mr. Mannering," said Eliza Doze, holding out a hand as if expecting him to kiss it. He held it lightly. Eliza glanced at the Sister in obvious dismissal, and when the door closed behind her, went on to Mannering, "I am very grateful to you for coming, sir."

"I'm sorry I didn't get here in time to stop the attack on you," Mannering said.

"If they hadn't caught me by surprise, *I* would have stopped them," she said, as if in no doubt of her ability to do just that. Such was her confidence that Mannering almost believed she could have done so.

Pulling a chair towards Eliza's bed, he sat down.

"Mrs. Doze—I wonder if you could tell me something

about those paintings of yours?" he asked. "How long have they been in your attic?"

The old woman flashed him a quick glance, then looked away. Her mouth tightened. It was almost as if she didn't want to tell him, reflected Mannering.

"Come on, Mrs. Doze," he persisted gently. "You must have some idea of how long they were there."

"Since—since my husband died." The words came out with a rush. "He always kept a lot of rubbish up in the attic, and after he passed on I didn't go up there very often. My one weak spot's my knees, sir. But Dr. Ignatzi found me some pills which took the pain away—for a little while, anyhow—so I went up to clear the rubbish. And there were the paintings, wrapped in some old sacks. Ezekiel—that was my husband, sir—must have put them there. Yes, *he* must have put them there." She leaned forward and lowered her voice. "Ezekiel was *cheated* by a dealer once, sir; absolutely robbed he was. I've never trusted dealers since."

"Then what made you trust me?"

"I was reading about you in a magazine," answered Eliza Doze. "You found a picture in a little village in Cornwall, and bought it for a song. Then you found it was worth a fortune. You shared what you got for it with the man you bought it from."

"But that was years ago!"

"My knees mightn't be so good, but there's naught the matter with my memory," said Eliza. "As a matter of fact, sir, it was just after Ezekiel had been defrauded, and we read about you together. 'Just my luck not to get a *good* dealer,' said Ezekiel. 'You mark my words,' I told him, 'there aren't many about like that Mr. Mannering.' If my Ezekiel were here now he'd say I was right, too."

"Mrs. Doze," said Mannering, "did anyone else ever go up into that attic?"

"Why should they?" the old lady demanded sharply.

"To fetch something for you, perhaps," suggested Mannering.

"The only one who ever went up there was Betsy, that's my grand-daughter," Eliza Doze declared.

"Did anyone ever break into the cottage?" asked Mannering.

"Not that I know of, sir, and who'd be more likely to know?"

"How often were you away from the cottage?"

"Twice a week regular, every Sunday and Wednesday," Eliza answered. "I go to one of my daughters in Salisbury one Wednesday, another daughter the next, my son's place the third and my sister's the fourth. I've done that for over ten years, sir."

"And where do you go on Sunday?"

"*Church*, sir." Eliza sounded reproachful. "Sunday morning that is. In the afternoon I go up to the Manor, my second cousin is head gardener there and I've always been up Sunday afternoons, even when Ezekiel was alive." The old woman wrinkled her forehead in a deep frown. "Are you suggesting someone might have broken in while I was *out*, Mr. Mannering?"

"I wondered," admitted Mannering.

"But why *should* they?"

"They could have been looking for old pictures."

Eliza Doze sniffed.

"Well, if they were, they never found none. I'll tell you who *did* come sneaking round, actually wanted to go up into the attic, only last week. That Jenkins at The Kettle. I soon sent *him* about his business."

"How did he know about the pictures?" asked Mannering.

"Betsy must have talked to his wife; Betsy always did talk too much. Not that she isn't a good girl, but anyone could make a fool of her!" Eliza Doze patted the side of her bed. "Come close, Mr. Mannering, will you please, sir?"

111

Mannering moved nearer, and Eliza leaned forward so that her lips were close to his ear. "If them pictures were not burnt, but robbed, and you finds 'em," she whispered, "and if as how they're worth a lot of money, Mr. Mannering, I want it to go to Miss Joanna. Not anything I've got in the post office or insurance, I've made a will for that, but anything from those pictures is Miss Joanna's."

"But Miss Joanna is a wealthy woman!" Mannering protested.

"That's what they *say*, but when you reach my age you've learnt you can't believe all you hear," went on Eliza in the same whispering voice. "*I* happen to know she's lost all her money, but she's a Cunliffe, too proud to admit loss to anyone. The money from those pictures is for *her*, Mr. Mannering. Promise me you'll see that she gets it."

"But you'll be able to see to that yourself," Mannering temporised.

"That's as maybe," said Eliza. "I want to be sure. Do you promise?"

Mannering hesitated.

He felt quite certain the paintings were those stolen from Colonel Cunliffe, and as soon as this whole mysterious affair was sorted out, they would have to be returned to him. Yet now, looking to Eliza's clear eyes, he thought that he saw supplication in them; this mattered a great deal to her.

"I promise that I'll do everything I can to help Miss Joanna," he said gently.

"Bless you, sir," said Eliza Doze, her voice very husky. "Bless you indeed, sir."

"But, Eliza——" Mannering hesitated, then took her hands, bony and skinny and speckled with brown. "What makes you think Joanna has lost all her money?"

"I *know* she has," insisted Eliza. "She's had to sell her

112

jewelry, she's had to sell nearly everything she owns. Why, she'd far rather leave the Manor and live in London, but she can't afford it. She told me so, Mr. Mannering. *She told me so.*"

CHAPTER FOURTEEN

MANNERING SEARCHES

It was after nine-thirty when Mannering reached the Manor. The lights were blazing, and there was an atmosphere of normality about the place that did not tally with what he knew. The front door was open, and as Mannering went in, Middleton appeared with the mysterious promptness of a good servant.

"Good evening, sir."

"Good evening, Middleton. Do you always leave the door unlocked as late as this?"

"Only when the Colonel is out, sir."

"I see."

"He sent his apologies, sir. He and Lady Markly are dining in Salisbury."

"Aren't I too late for dinner?"

"No, sir," said Middleton. "The Colonel doesn't like set times for guests."

"I'll be down in twenty minutes," Mannering promised.

"Very good, sir."

Mannering went up to his room, and put in a call to Larraby, who lived in a bachelor apartment above Quinns. In little more than a few seconds, Larraby was on the line.

"Good evening, sir."

"Josh, I want Beverley Willis's home number, quickly."

"It's in my book, sir, if you will wait one moment—ah, Flaxman 73551. He lives near King's Road and Cheyne Walk—very close to you, sir."

"Thanks. And Josh—I want you to come to Salisbury first thing in the morning."

"I could drive down at once," offered Larraby.

Mannering hesitated, and then said: "That might be a good idea." He paused. "No—better make a really early start tomorrow. I'll meet you at the Red Lion at eight o'clock, and we'll have some breakfast."

"Very good, sir. Am I to understand some kind of emergency has arisen?"

"You are indeed," Mannering told him. "Make sure you're not followed, and be very careful."

"I'm sorry it's like that sir. Shall I tell Mrs. Mannering not to expect you tomorrow?"

"Yes," Mannering said. "Has anything cropped up in London?"

"M. Corot telephoned from Paris to confirm that he cannot go to South America, and hopes very much that you can."

"So do I," said Mannering, "but don't commit me yet."

He rang off, and waited for a few seconds before picking up the receiver. He could not be sure that the line was untapped but heard nothing to suggest that it was. He put in the call to Flaxman 73551 and a masculine voice with a faintly Scottish accent answered.

"I'm sorry, Mr. Willis is out and I cannot be sure when he will be home."

"Tell him I called and will call again in the morning, will you? This is John Mannering."

"Be sure I will tell him, Mr. Mannering."

Mannering put down the receiver, changed his shirt and tie and went down to dinner. It was strange, almost

115

eerie to be in the big dining room by himself. Middleton and a young maid waited on him, and at the end of a meal of simple excellence, Mannering asked:

"Where is Anstiss tonight?"

"It's his night off duty, sir."

"I see. Don't wait up for me if I go out again, I'll take a key."

"Very good, sir," Middleton said, unsurprised.

At half-past ten, Mannering left in the hired car, driving towards the main road, watchful for the slightest sign of an attack. There was none. At the road he turned left, away from Salisbury, driving for half a mile or so, until he came to a less known entrance to the Manor. He turned into this, put out his headlights and drove slowly until he could see the lights of the main house. He parked on the grass verge, and walked slowly forward. No one was about. He entered by the side door and went up a secondary staircase to the main landing, sure that no one had seen him. He stopped at Joanna's door, tried the handle and pushed.

The door was locked.

Who would lock it, when Joanna was away?

Mannering took out his penknife and used a picklock swiftly and dexterously. After only a few seconds the lock clicked back. The room was in darkness when he stepped inside. He put on the light, checked the door to make sure that no light would shine through to the landing, and began to search the room. He found a jewel box on the dressing-table but it contained only a few oddments of costume jewelry. Opening a drawer, he discovered a bank statement which showed that Joanna was about four hundred pounds overdrawn—an indication that Eliza Doze might be right. Beneath it, among some typewritten letters, was one from a Salisbury bank.

Dear Miss Cunliffe,

I will appreciate it if you will call and see me one

day in the near future. I am sure that you understand that we do not wish to cause you any inconvenience but if you wish to continue the assistance we have been glad to arrange I hope it will be possible for you to offer some security.

This badly phrased letter was obviously written by a man who felt ill-at-ease about making such an approach to this particular client. It was crystal clear that Joanna had been overdrawn for some time.

Then Mannering came upon a letter which startled him. Dated five years earlier, it read:

Dear Joanna,

As your mother's friend as well as her legal adviser I want you to know that I will assist you in any way I can. I have already told you how deeply grieved I am about your mother's death, but please believe that I want very much to help for your own sake, not simply for your mother's memory.

You are very young; it will be three years and more before you come into the very large sum that you inherit from your mother. As a trustee, I can assure you that the inheritance will be wisely administered, and if you have any special personal need of money, it will, of course, be made available.

Yours very sincerely,
Martin C. Wilberforce

"A very large sum," Mannering murmured to himself. "How large, I wonder?" He went through more of the papers, and then came upon a letter from a different manager of the same bank.

Dear Miss Cunliffe,

Thank you for your letter. I am indeed glad to continue to handle your account and the bank's services

117

as well as our advice are always at your disposal. I am enclosing a copy of the list of securities lodged with us and will be glad if you will sign one copy and return it to us.

The other copy was attached.

The total value of cash and securities was over fifteen thousand pounds.

"Can *that* have gone in two years?" Mannering asked aloud.

He finished his search. There were a few bank statements of recent date showing an overdraft, which would not have mattered but for the specific request for security.

If a girl of twenty-three had gone through that amount of money in two years, what had she spent it on? If she *had* been blackmailed, it must have been for something pretty serious.

He put all the papers back where he had found them, then stood by the door and surveyed the room. He could think of nothing he had missed until he caught sight of a handbag on a small table. He stepped across, picked this up and opened it.

Inside were a few oddments, a little money, some keys and a folded note which read: *Don't play around any longer. We mean business.*

Mannering had never seen a more obvious blackmail ultimatum. He refolded it carefully, holding it by the edges as he slipped it inside an envelope which he placed in his pocket. Then he switched off the light, waiting for a few seconds before opening the door. No one was outside. He went down the secondary staircase and into the grounds by the side entrance, walking through the garden towards the cottage where Lady Markly lived. Mannering didn't really believe she had anything to do with the missing paintings; nevertheless, with so much unsolved mystery, anything was possible, and this would be an excellent opportunity to search the cottage.

Walking up to the cottage, he circled it, then stood for a moment motionless in the shadows. There were no lights in the windows, front or back. No one appeared to have followed him, nor was there any sound of movement. Stepping inside the tiny porch, he began to work on the lock of the cottage door with a piece of specially toughened steel. Practised as he was, it made very little noise; nevertheless he paused again, to make sure no one had been disturbed, before pushing the door open. He switched on a pocket torch and the beam stabbed like a white dagger through the darkness. Through the hall he crept, past the tiny kitchen, and into the room beyond.

This really was a tiny place; he should be through in fifteen minutes, perhaps even ten. He moved forward as he shone the torch ahead—and kicked against something unyielding on the floor. He struck it so heavily that he tripped and fell, wrenching his shoulder, the torch weaving a wild pattern on the opposite wall.

He put the torch out and got to his feet in darkness, listening, heart thumping.

There was no sound.

He switched on the torch again and, almost fearfully, directed it downwards.

It flickered across a pair of highly polished black shoes, along a pair of trousered legs, a white shirt front, a bow-tie—a face.

It shone on the face of Anstiss, thief and footman.

Mannering was quite sure that Anstiss was dead, although he could not see immediately what had caused death. The man lay on his back, his head turned to one side. His mouth was slack, his eyes were nearly closed.

Slowly Mannering groped for, and found, his wrist; the pulse was still.

He straightened up and leaned against the wall, breathing heavily. The sensible thing was to get away at once, before anyone discovered him here—and yet he wanted to search the cottage. Once the body was found the police would take over, and there would be no chance at all to make a search.

The curtains were drawn.

He shone the torch towards the door until it showed the light switch, crossed to it and flicked it down. The light fell on a charmingly furnished sitting-cum-dining room. His gaze passed over a settee, two easy chairs, a small table, and came to rest on a writing-bureau. It was unlocked, but contained nothing to give him any help, only the kind of business documents that a woman living alone would have.

She had a bank balance of eight hundred and seven pounds and a deposit account of a little over a thousand; hardly a fortune. She appeared to own a few building society shares and a few other securities, but she wasn't a wealthy woman, on this evidence.

It was time he went.

Putting out the light, he went back into the hall and crept swiftly up the narrow, carpeted stairs. After a quick look round the tiny bedroom, he lifted the curtain, not expecting to see anything but the lights of the Manor and the shapes of trees.

He stood appalled.

Not far off were two police cars, their headlights pointing towards the cottage. Half a dozen men had alighted. Mannering saw the beams of other cars, the shapes of other men, turned in the same direction. The cottage was surrounded by the police; he had no chance to get away.

Shocked, aghast, Mannering let the curtain fall. He could hear no sounds, for the men approached across grass, but it would not be more than two minutes before they reached the door.

120

Who had sent for them?

That thought passed through his mind as he went towards the landing, reached it and looked upwards. There, as he had hoped, he saw a hatch to an attic. He measured the distance with his eyes, and jumped, hands banging upwards, knocking the hatch cover to one side. Then he jumped again, gripped the edge of the hatch and hauled himself up, the pain in his shoulder almost unbearable. Yet he was able to climb through, scrambling over the side, then to push the hatch cover into place. It fell with a click.

He had won a few minutes' respite.

Was there an attic window? The roof was of thatch, he remembered, but he had never been near the cottage by day. Cautiously he flicked the torch; the beam fell coldly, impartially, on two paintings. He caught his breath.

These were the paintings he had taken from the studio, and which had been stolen in turn from the Mini after the crash.

He paused long enough to make doubly sure, then shone the torch about the attic. The sloping roof reached to the floor on either side, and even in the middle there was hardly room to stand upright.

There *was* a window, small but big enough for him to squeeze through, giving him hope that there was still a chance of getting out on to the roof and dropping down to safety.

The alternative was to open the door when the knocking began, to tell the truth and hope that the police would believe him. Surely no one in their senses would seriously believe that *he* had murdered Anstiss!

But whether they did or not, the police would have to hold him, and he would be able to do nothing more to help Joanna. He had a mental picture of Joanna, pale and still, and of Dr. Ignatzi, deeply worried because he believed that someone had poisoned the girl.

The choice was already made; he had to try to get away. If he failed and were caught, then he cou'd tell the truth; there would be almost as much hope of being believed then as now.

Wedging the two pictures inside his jacket, he edged towards the window.

CHAPTER FIFTEEN

FIRE! FIRE!

From the window Mannering could see two of the cars, the beams of their headlights very bright. He noticed with relief that they were focussed no higher than the ground floor. He also saw the men halfway between the cars and the cottage, approaching with great caution; others hovered near the cars, and it was more likely that behind the lights were still more.

Once outside, he could crouch on the window recess, for the window, a dormer type, was built deep into the thatch. Not until he dropped upright was he likely to be seen—though there was always the possibility that some-one would take a single glance upwards and raise the alarm. But this was a chance he would have to take.

Once out of the window, where should he go?

He saw the wire netting which covered the thatch to keep the birds from nesting. So thatch and wire would give him some kind of hold.

He would have to climb out backwards.

With two sound shoulders he would not have given the risk a moment's thought. Now, flexing the sound one, he opened the window to its widest extent and began to ease himself through. As he did so, he heard a banging from below; the police were at the front door of the cottage, and would probably break in at any moment.

He heard a shout.

Had they seen him?

He could not hope to get away if they had.

He lowered his legs so that soon the lower part of his body was resting against the roof, the top half on the window ledge, head still inside the room. The banging was repeated; so was the shout, but he could not distinguish any words.

He heard a car horn blare.

He edged himself to one side, and at last was outside the window, spreadeagled, his feet overhanging the thatch, his fingers entwined in the wire; at least there was little risk of falling.

More shouting came.

My God! They were shouting: *"Fire, fire!"*

He heard more car horns and an excited babble of voices, with the single word *fire* repeated over and over again. Still edging away from the window, terrifyingly aware that the fire must be in the cottage or there wouldn't be so much excitement, he could look neither down nor behind him.

He had a vivid recollection of Eliza Doze's roof disappearing in wild billows of smoke; could almost hear the roaring of the flames and see the lurid glow.

There *was* a red glow—on the right.

Near by was a big tree, one branch almost touching him. A flickering red light danced on the leaves.

Someone bellowed: *"Get back. Get back!"*

Someone else called clearly: "Get those people away!"

Another car was approaching, and a man spoke in a tone of alarm.

"There's Colonel Cunliffe! . . . And Lady Markly."

Mannering could hear these voices as he edged away from the window. The fire was fierce enough now for the glow to be reflected on the tree and back on to him. *He could feel the heat.* He glanced towards the tree and saw the big overhanging bough only two or three feet away from him.

Would it support his weight?

At least it would hide him.

He dropped his legs over the edge of the roof, and at arm's length was only a few feet off the ground. Swinging his body as far as it would go, he lurched sideways, falling almost directly beneath that big branch. He heard the roaring of fire and the honking of horns as he staggered up, leaves and twigs brushing his head and face. He could see the huge trunk of the tree in the red glow, rounded it, and kept moving. If he had to run for it, it would be the end; he was already gasping for breath, his damaged shoulder aching badly.

No one seemed to look his way.

He broke cover of the branches, stealthily. Now the whole of the grounds seemed to be illuminated in that ominous red light, and he felt the stench of smoke in his nostrils. He could see a car and a group of people to the right, but no one was in front of him. He quickened his pace and reached a spot behind the quickly gathering crowd. Soon, he was near the side entrance of the Manor. The lights were on, and the door was wide open, but no one was about. He went in, walking swiftly up the secondary staircase.

A woman nearby said: "What a frightful thing."

"That's the second one," Betsy Doze said tearfully. "The second one."

Mannering reached his own room and went inside.

This time, he put the two canvases behind the wardrobe. Then he undressed, bathed, brushed the leaves and straw out of his hair, put on pyjamas and got into bed. At the last moment he remembered to set his alarm for seven o'clock.

He would probably be disturbed before that, anyhow. But no one disturbed him, and he woke to the alarm.

For several minutes he lay on his back, staring at the shaft of sunlight on the ceiling. Then he rang the bell, and in a few moments Betsy Doze came in with tea. She wore the pale blue linen dress that was the uniform of the maids at the Manor.

"Hallo, Betsy! So you work here now?"

"Just temporary, sir," Betsy said, putting the tray on the bedside table. "Oh, you *are* lucky!"

"What am I lucky about?" asked Mannering.

"Sleeping through it all."

"All through what?"

"The fire, sir!"

Once she had started, there was no stopping her, and Mannering learned that the cottage had been gutted "*Just like Gran's*" and that all Lady Markly's lovely possessions had been lost.

She went away at last, excited as much as perturbed.

Mannering got up, bathed, found his shoulder much less uncomfortable than he had feared, and at twenty minutes to eight went out, taking Joanna's two pictures with him. There was no sign of Middleton. He wondered whether the police knew that there had been a body in that cottage—even whether they would ever know.

It was a crisp, bright morning, after a heavy dew.

He drove towards the highway, seeing no one at work, no one in sight, until he reached the drive gates. A policeman stood there squarely blocking his path.

Mannering stopped—and recognised the man whom he had seen on the evening of the first fire.

"Good morning, sir." The man peered through the car window. "Oh, it's Mr. Mannering. Are you leaving for good. sir?"

"No. I'm going to Salisbury to meet the manager of my London shop."

126

"I see, sir. I have to report all movements in and out of the Manor," the policeman went on. "You weren't at the fire last night, sir, were you?"

"No, I was tired out after a rough day, and slept like a log, but I've heard all about it."

The policeman shook his head. "There's some talk of a man being burned alive."

"Oh, no!" exclaimed Mannering, and had a quick mental glimpse of Anstiss, lying still and dead.

"Yes, sir. A man was seen going into the cottage only half an hour or so before the fire," the constable added. "We went to get him as a matter of fact, sir."

"And he didn't get away?"

"No one saw him leave and the cottage was surrounded," announced the constable, not without relish.

"Very nasty indeed," said Mannering.

He drove on, wondering why the police had gathered in such strength outside the cottage and reflecting wryly that he himself could easily have been burned alive. Now that he was wide awake he opened his mind to urgent questions: who had started that fire, and why?

Anstiss, he knew, was a fire-raiser. Had he planted a petrol-incendiary and then been attacked and murdered? Or had his killer left an incendiary so as to destroy the body and conceal the murder?

There were really three questions. Who had killed Anstiss? Who had set fire to the cottage? And why had the police arrived so promptly and in such strength?

He was turning towards the Market Square when he passed a police car; in it was Chief Inspector Fishlock. Fishlock, recognizing him, nodded. A minute late Mannering pulled up outside the Red Lion Hotel. He parked almost at the entrance, passed under the hanging creeper which gave the inn its special charm and went into the small hallway which had not been altered substantially from the days when the Red Lion had been a coaching inn.

Josh Larraby and Beverley Willis were standing by a huge, carved grandfather clock.

Mannering shook hands, while Larraby said: "We arranged for breakfast in a private room, Mr. Mannering; we thought we could talk more freely there. Willis drove me down," he added. A waiter appeared, elderly, affable, and led them back across the courtyard and into a big room with chairs all about the sides, odd tables, and one set for breakfast in a corner away from the window.

"And I ordered porridge, bacon, eggs and sausages, and coffee," Larraby went on.

Mannering chuckled.

"That sounds fine. I'm glad you're here too, Willis, I wanted to have a word with you. Phoned you last night, as a matter of fact. But what made you come?"

"Hester Cunliffe," replied Willis, languidly, but the expression in his brown eyes was intent. There was something unusually attractive about his saturnine face, his delusive foppishness and lean figure. "She talked to her father on the telephone yesterday and he told her about Joanna. How *is* Joanna, sir?"

"I haven't inquired this morning, but she'll be all right. Did Colonel Cunliffe mention that it looked as if someone tried to murder her?"

"Good God! No!"

"That's what it does look like," Mannering said. He paused as the waiter hovered over them, changing plates, and continued after the man had gone: "Willis, how much do you know about Joanna?"

"Not very much, in fact," answered Willis. "I've known her on and off since she was at school, but she's younger than Hester and—but she's a very nice person, sir."

128

"Has Hester ever said she was worried—that Joanna was worried, I mean?"

They were eating.

"She's often said *she* was worried about Joanna; she seemed to think something was wrong. For one thing Joanna always appeared to be short of money, although she inherited quite a lot from her mother. Hester thinks she may have made some foolish investments."

"Any men in her life?"

"I shouldn't think so," said Willis, reflectively.

"I want you to find out," Mannering said. "Can you talk to Hester this evening?"

"No trouble about that!"

"And I want to know if Hester knows of anything which happened about a year ago and affected Joanna or her father," Mannering went on. "It looks as if she's being very cruelly blackmailed. Any love affairs, misdemeanors, anything which would give anyone power over Joanna? See what I'm after?"

"Only too clearly," Willis said, unhappily.

"Ask Hester to tell you everything she possibly can," added Mannering. He paused and looked very earnestly into the younger man's eyes. "It could mean the difference between life and death for Joanna."

"If there's anything at all Hester can do, she will," Willis said confidently. "She plans to come down for the weekend, but if it would help she could get off today."

"I think that might complicate things," Mannering answered. "I'll telephone if there seems any need. And now"—he turned to Larraby—"I've a couple of modern pictures which have been painted over older ones. I want you to examine them very closely—the new work and the old. The old ones may be very old indeed." He did not say that he thought Joanna might have painted over stolen pictures; there was a limit to how much he wanted

129

to confide in Beverley Willis. "And I want to know as much about Harry Anstiss as you can find out."

"I've a complete dossier," Larraby said, picking up his brief-case. "It isn't *very* different from the one on the man Jenkins. Both are knowledgeable about old paintings, each has been a runner for most of his life, each has served two prison sentences for theft." He took out a folder and placed it in Mannering's hands.

"Thanks," Mannering said, appreciatively. "Anything here about his associates?"

"Nothing very much," said Larraby, "but he's worked with one man on and off for years—I learned this from Mendlesohn." Mendlesohn was a picture restorer and framer whose knowledge of the business was almost inexhaustible. "A man named White, who sometimes calls himself Cobb, and sometimes Lobb." Larraby was speaking with great precision. "I'm wondering if this is *your* Lobb, sir."

"Sounds like it," said Mannering. "What do you know about him?"

"Only that he has been known to extort blackmail, sir; and that his knowledge of painting is extensive."

"And you really think that Joanna is being blackmailed!" exclaimed Willis. "Why, it's incredible!"

"That's what we have to find out," Mannering said, cautiously. He took the blackmail note which he had found in Joanna's bedroom from his pocket-book, and passed it to Larraby. "Check this, will you, Josh—I think hou'll find it's been written by our friend Lobb. And now," he added, "you'd better be on your way. Be careful with those pictures, and watch for trouble on the road."

"Do you seriously think there might be any, sir?" asked Larraby.

"Very seriously," said Mannering gravely.

Ten minutes later, Larraby and Willis drove off in Willis's TR3.

Fifteen minutes later, as Mannering was paying the bill, Chief Inspector Fishlock entered the hotel.

"I'd like to talk to you, Mr. Mannering," he said, without preamble. "At once please." Something in his manner was ominous, almost threatening. "Here or at the station; it doesn't matter where, to begin with."

CHAPTER SIXTEEN

THE INFORMER

Mannering finished with the cashier, turned and smiled at Fishlock, and saw two couples approaching the reception desk, obviously hotel visitors. But he stayed where he was.

"What can I do for you, Inspector?" he asked mildly.

Curious glances turned towards them.

"Hadn't we better find somewhere private?"

"It's up to you," Mannering said. "I want to go round to The Kettle. How far is it?"

"I'll drive you," offered Fishlock, "and one of my chaps can follow in your car."

As soon as it was settled, Fishlock turned to Mannering, his expression the portentous one of a man about to deliver a broadside. "Now, sir—what were you doing in Lady Markly's cottage last night?"

Obviously, he expected the question to shatter Mannering's calm; certainly he was surprised by Mannering's chuckle.

"So you learned about that!"

"You don't deny it?"

"I don't see why I should," said Mannering, as they moved off.

"Why didn't you tell us?"

Mannering smiled. "You didn't ask me."

"That is simply begging the question, sir."

"I suppose it is," conceded Mannering, glancing at the other's stern, set face, "but I had quite a day yesterday, Chief Inspector. Attempts on one's life, foiled by a hair's breadth, don't leave much energy to face an interrogation. You were bound to want to ask a lot of questions, and I was too tired."

"Were you in the cottage when it was set alight?"

"I was there when it burst into flames," Mannering answered. "I got out through the attic window, and to the best of my knowledge, no one saw me."

A quick look at the Inspector told Mannering he was giving nothing away.

"It was your duty to report to us."

"I'm sorry if I've offended you," said Mannering soothingly.

"It's not a question of offending me, it——" Fishlock hesitated and then relaxed a little. "Why did you go there?"

"To see what I could find."

"What *did* you find?"

"Nothing of any consequence."

"You are aware that you committed an infraction of law?"

"Technically, yes."

"Mr. Mannering. You may have a remarkable reputation in London, but here——"

Mannering broke across his words sharply.

"I'm not happy about what's happening down here, Chief Inspector. At least one of the Cunliffe staff is a known criminal——"

"Which one?" interrupted Fishlock.

"The footman—Anstiss."

"We were on to him," Fishlock said with satisfaction. "He seems to have realized it."

"You are sure?"

"He's missing this morning."

So the police had not been able to identify the dead man, thought Mannering. All the same, they were bound to make intensive investigations. Perhaps it would be best, while not breaking his word to Colonel Cunliffe, to tell Fishlock part at least of what had been going on at Nether Manor. He was still turning this over in his mind as Fishlock asked abruptly:

"Who came to see you here this morning?"

"The manager of my London shop, and an assistant."

"May I ask why?"

"I wanted to see them. I wanted information about Anstiss, Jenkins of The Kettle, and a man named White *alias* Cobb *alias* Lobb. Chief Inspector, I have very strong suspicions that these three men are involved in a pretty nasty art fraud. And I think they know that I'm on to them, and that is why I was run down by that lorry."

"Assuming you're right, sir are you sure it was you they meant to run down?" demanded Fishlock, and when Mannering showed some surprise, went on: "How do you know it wasn't an attempt to kill Colonel Cunliffe, who often used that particular car?"

Mannering drew a deep breath.

"I don't know," he admitted. "I hadn't even thought of it. Do you think Cunliffe is in danger?"

"He could be. Mr. Mannering——" Fishlock paused.

"Yes."

"Did you know where the Colonel and Lady Markly were last night?"

"I didn't see the Colonel yesterday evening—I was in late—but Middleton told me that he and Lady Markly were dining in Salisbury."

"They had planned to dine at Lady Markly's cottage," Fishlock announced, "but changed plans at the last moment and dined at The Haunch of Venison. Whoever started that fire may well have known that they *were* to have been at the cottage. It could easily have been an attempt to murder Colonel Cunliffe. Do you see *that*, Mr. Mannering?"

"All too clearly, Chief Inspector. However, I did not set fire to the cottage. Indeed, I came within an ace of dying in the fire myself. You can't have it both ways."

"And nor can you, sir. You can't have the co-operation and protection of the police unless you confide in them. *Why* did you go to Lady Markly's cottage? What in particular did you hope to find?" When Mannering didn't answer Fishlock went on with great deliberation: "Mr. Mannering, the Cunliffe family has a great deal of influence and can call on a great deal of loyalty in this part of Wiltshire. We have suspected for some time that something abnormal has been going on here, but the local people won't talk. There is no reason for you to keep anything to yourself for the sake of the family, is there?"

"None at all." Mannering was sorry to have to lie, but he had, he reminded himself, given his promise to Colonel Cunliffe.

"Then perhaps we can make a bargain, Mr. Mannering. You tell us why you went to the cottage last night and we will postpone any charge of burglarious entry until we have had a chance to check your story. But don't lose any more time, sir. This is going to be a very busy day."

Mannering studied the strong face and the set expression, and took a very real liking to Chief Inspector Fishlock.

"I agree with you on the probable busyness of the day, Chief Inspector, but what do you stand to gain if you charge me? You couldn't make a charge of fire-raising; in spite of my admission of guilt you can't prove I was there. You might possibly hold me in custody overnight but by tomorrow I'd get bail. All you would do would be to take me out of circulation for twelve hours or so, during which time I couldn't talk to Jenkins, Colonel

Cunliffe, Lady Markly or any of the staff, each of whom might give something away." Mannering paused. "I won't run, I promise you—I'll stay here until this is all over."

"What do you hope to achieve?" Fishlock demanded.

"I hope to find the answers."

"What do you stand to gain from doing so? There's no personal reason why you should risk your life, is there?"

"None."

"Then why *do* you, sir?"

"My wife often asks the same question," said Mannering mildly. "She can't understand what makes me enjoy mountaineering, what makes me enjoy confrontations with criminals, what makes me carry a tool-kit and nylon rope, both highly suspicious in the eyes of the police. I don't even understand myself, Chief Inspector. But I don't like art treasures being stolen and smuggled and treated as if their only value was the price they fetch, I don't like attacks on my life, and I don't like attacks on young women. These dislikes get me into many tight corners—as happened last night. Luckily, I've trained myself to get out of them and to use equipment which helps." He paused, then added drily: "I hope that helps you, Chief Inspector."

"Do you know," Fishlock said in a gruff amazement, "I *believe* you!"

Mannering chuckled. "Most policemen do after a while, but you've been much quicker than most. Now—let's make a bargain, Chief Inspector. You give me any help I need, and twenty-four hours from now I'll tell you everything I know or think I know."

"So you can put a time limit on to it."

"I think so."

"How is that, sir?"

"I've been involved in a great number of investigations into art frauds, and the time always comes when the criminals realize that the game's nearly up. Some just

136

cave in. Some slip away quietly. Some make a big effort at a final killing. This is likely to be one of the last. The man Lobb is a killer type. If my suspicions are correct, he's fighting you, me and probably someone else whom we don't know, as if his back were to the wall. That makes him doubly dangerous. Do you see what I mean?"

"I see that it doubles the danger to anyone who gets in his way."

"Probably."

"Yet you'll still go on?"

"Do you turn your back on a case because you might get hurt?" asked Mannering.

"No, sir," said Fishlock. There was a short pause before he added: "Why do you want to see Jenkins at The Kettle?"

"He might have information for me. He asked me to come down about Eliza Doze's pictures."

"So he knew about them," mused Fishlock. "I can't imagine Eliza Doze being involved in crime—but you never know. This man Lobb, now. Are you sure he's dangerous?"

"Deadly."

"Can you prove it?"

"I hope so."

Fishlock frowned. "If he doesn't kill you first?"

"If he tries again we might catch him red-handed," remarked Mannering.

They had both tacitly dropped the possibility that Cunliffe, not Mannering, had been the intended victim.

Five minutes later, deeply thoughtful, Fishlock pulled up in a street not far from the cathedral. Mannering's gray Ford Cortina, driven by a police sergeant, pulled up behind him. From a wrought-iron arm attached to a nearby shop, hung, like an inn sign, a big copper kettle.

"Thank you, Chief Inspector. And you, too, Sergeant." Mannering took the ignition keys the sergeant held out to him.

"I hope neither of us is going to regret this," Fishlock said grimly.

Mannering paused for a moment to watch the two men drive off, then turned into the shop. It was small and gloomy, but as his eyes became accustomed to the dim light he saw the burnished sides of old copper and brass pans, a good display of pewter and some china figures that would grace any drawing-room. There were a few old prints and two or three paintings hanging on the walls. A door at the back of the shop was open and a woman appeared.

She was young and attractive in a modern way, with a sheath dress and straight hair hanging to her shoulders. If this was Jenkins's wife Dora, Jenkins was a lucky man.

"Yes, sir?"

"Is Mr. Jenkins in?" asked Mannering.

"No, I'm afraid not. He's away on business. I'm his wife—can I help?"

"He asked me to come down and see some paintings."

"Are you Mr. *Mannering?*" Her voice rose.

"Yes."

"I'm sorry, Mr. Mannering, but my husband phoned a message to you only last night, to say he'd been detained on business in London. And he asked me to tell you that the paintings he thought would interest you weren't on the market any longer." She spoke definitely, as if determined to convince him.

"Well, it can't be helped," Mannering said. "But now I'm here I may as well look round."

"You—you won't be long, will you?" She looked anxious, but it was an anxiety she hoped to conceal.

"Only a few minutes," Mannering promised.

"I've got to close the shop while I go and do some shopping you see, sir."

"In that case, I'd better not wait," Mannering said, and half turned towards the street door. He actually took a step towards it, followed by Dora Jenkins, then suddenly

138

swung round, pushed past her and strode into the room beyond.

Lobb stood behind the door. He had a spiked stick in his hand, raised to strike.

Mrs. Jenkins gave a shrill squeak, but whether in protest or terror it was hard to say.

Lobb looked at Mannering, raising the stick a few inches higher. The woman gasped. Mannering did not move.

"This time you've had it, Mannering," growled Lobb.

"Percy—Percy, *don't!*" breathed the woman.

"You've really had it," Lobb repeated. He began to swing the stick as if he were going to throw it. "Close the door, Dora."

"Percy, you can't——"

"Go and close the front door and put the *Closed* sign up."

Mannering heard the woman's agitated breathing, then heard her footsteps.

"Why waste a perfectly good door?" he said clearly. "The police will only knock it down if it's locked."

The footsteps hesitated, stopped.

"He's bluffing," Lobb sneered. "Don't move, Mannering. Lock the door and put the sign up, Dora."

She was half crying as she moved further away, but Mannering felt sure she would do what she was told. She was well inside the shop now and Mannering heard the door swing to, heard the lock click, then the bolt shoot home. He had not moved since he had stepped into the inner room, but now he turned to face his adversary.

"You're a fool, Lobb." He spoke dispassionately.

Lobb grunted, nonplussed, a little wary.

"You're a fool," Mannering repeated. "You can kill too often."

"What the hell do you mean?"

"There's a little story about a man who kills the goose that lays the golden eggs; you might read it to your advantage," Mannering suggested. "Why don't you start thinking?"

"Thinking?" echoed Lobb, in a tone of disbelief.

"*Thinking*. You know who I am, don't you?"

"I know you're Mannering of Quinns."

"Quinns have five branches throughout the world, and more means of disposing of old masters than any other single company," Mannering said. "And Quinns is trusted by all the big collectors and the big dealers. You'll do a lot better for yourself if you come to terms with me than you will if you kill me and sell where you can."

"You're offering me a *deal*?" asked Lobb slowly.

"Why do you think I came down here?" demanded Mannering. "And why do you think I came into The Kettle? If it comes to that, why did I take the paintings Anstiss stole and hide them away? When are you going to wake up, Lobb?"

There was a long pause.

Then Lobb threw back his head and roared with laughter.

CHAPTER SEVENTEEN

RUN WITH THE HARE . . .

Dora Jenkins moved from the shop towards Mannering and Lobb, staring at Mannering as if at a worker of miracles. Lobb's laughter echoed and re-echoed, and pewter and brass quivered musically on the walls and shelves. Dora's face gradually cleared, and she began to smile; she had a deep dimple in her right cheek.

At last, Lobb stopped laughing. "So you run with the hare"—he guffawed again, and his whole body went limp—"and hunt with the hounds!"

"When it suits me."

"And it suits you now, although it didn't before."

"If you've a proposition to make it worth my while, it suits me now," Mannering said. "I'm not cheap."

"My God, Dora," Lobb said. "D'you hear him? Run with the hare . . . What do you know about this business, Mannering?"

"I know that you think it's worth murder."

"*No!*" gasped Dora.

"You tried to kill me, you tried to kill Joanna and you did kill Anstiss," Mannering said quite clearly.

"Percy——!"

"Don't take any notice of Mannering's careless talk.

141

Go into the kitchen and start cooking my breakfast," Lobb ordered sharply.

"Percy, you didn't kill——!"

"Do what I say."

She moved slowly towards a doorway at the back of this inner room, gave a final glance over her shoulder and disappeared. Lobb moved across and closed the door.

"Don't you know better than to talk in front of a woman?" Lobb demanded.

"Don't you know better than to get a woman to telephone the police that I was at the cottage last night?" countered Mannering, testing out a lightning suspicion and seeing by Lobb's expression that he was right.

"Who told you she——?"

"A woman telephoned Fishlock. Who else would it be but Dora?" When Lobb didn't answer, Mannering went on: "Five minutes' questioning, and she would admit she did it."

"That's as maybe." Lobb's voice was harsh now, all trace of laughter gone. "Who said I killed Anstiss?"

"I do."

"Prove it."

"Lobb, or Cobb, or White, if you prefer it—if I have to prove it, it will be to the police. Chief Inspector Fishlock just dropped me outside, by the way—and if I should fail to leave, he will certainly want to know why."

"I saw him," Lobb muttered. "Why have *him* to drive you around?"

"I told him I was going to look into all the antique shops in the way of business," Mannering said. "*He* told *me* that Jenkins had served time. Don't run away with the idea that the local police are stupid."

"They're stupid all right," said Lobb, harshly. He fell silent for a while and Mannering kept silent too. "So you know Anstiss is dead," he added at last.

"I saw him at the cottage."

"How do you know the police won't suspect 'you?"

"They can suspect whom they like; what matters is that I can prove he was dead when I got there"—would his bluff work? wondered Mannering—"and alive when he was there with you. Why did you kill him?"

"The same reason I would kill anybody," blustered Lobb. "I didn't trust him. And I'm not sure I trust you."

Mannering shrugged. "You don't have to."

"And you don't know as much as you think you do," sneered Lobb. "I didn't try to kill Joanna Cunliffe."

"Who did?"

"I don't know who did."

"Why try to kill me?"

"I didn't want you around," Lobb said. "You could have discovered too much."

"Didn't it occur to you to ask me if I would do a deal?"

"No," Lobb answered frankly. "I thought you were one of those Holy Joes who wouldn't even cheat the Customs. You still could be," he added sharply.

"You're right," Mannering said. "So I could."

"How much *do* you know?" demanded Lobb.

"Apart from the fact that you killed Anstiss and tried to kill me, I know you've been operating with Joanna for a year," Mannering told him. "I know you've got the girl where you want her, I know she's paid you a fortune during that year, I know you use Anstiss and Jenkins to sell your pictures—and I know I would get twice as much for any I sold, probably three or four times as much." Mannering moved across to the wall and examined a picture that was propped against it, then turned back to his companion. "When do we start talking business?"

Lobb frowned. "How do I know you're on the level?"

"You don't, but I can prove it."

"Tell me how."

143

"Give me a worthwhile picture—or anything worthwhile to sell," Mannering said reasonably. "You don't have to tell me its history."

Lobb was breathing very heavily.

"So I give you a piece of stolen property and you turn it in to the police. It's not *that* easy, Mannering."

Mannering shrugged.

"Who said it was easy?" He turned towards the door leading back to the shop. "I'm going to see the other antique people," he added. "I should think it will take me about two hours." He had his back to Lobb, and was speaking very casually. "I hope you'll have made up your mind by then."

He walked through the shop towards the street door.

"Mannering!" called Lobb.

Mannering paused. "Well?"

"You could turn me in."

Mannering slipped a hand into his pocket. "My car's across the road—a gray Ford Cortina." He took out his keys and tossed them towards Lobb. "Put anything you like in there, and I'll do what I can with it. Lock the stuff in the boot, and leave the keys on the dashboard shelf."

He opened the street door and went out.

Soon, he was in another antique shop near by, looking round the well-filled rooms and the attractively displayed stock. Prices were high for a provincial town, but he raised no questions except to ask where the next antique shop was. He visited five altogether and it took him an hour and three-quarters. Passing the Red Lion Hotel, he had coffee in a tea-room attached, then walked back to The Kettle. He went in, the bell clanged and almost immediately Dora Jenkins appeared from the back.

Mannering smiled brightly.

"Is Mr. Lobb in?"

"No, he's gone out. He—he's my brother!" she announced breathlessly. "And he didn't kill anybody!"

"That's good," Mannering said.

"You shouldn't have said he did."

"So he told me. I'm sorry. Where is he, Mrs. Jenkins?"

"He's gone out," she repeated. "He'll telephone you at the Manor tonight."

"I see," Mannering said. "Dora, don't get mixed up in his affairs. He may be your brother but he's a very dangerous man."

"You think I don't know it?" she answered, her voice tinged with bitterness. "You're a fine one to talk!" she added sharply.

"I can look after myself, Dora, but you can't."

"I do all right!" she muttered.

Mannering shrugged, and went out.

He drove through the city, twice getting lost because of the one-way streets, then called at the Infirmary, where he was told that there was no change in Joanna's condition but that Eliza Doze would be discharged the next day. Getting back into the car, he drove towards the Manor and did not stop until he was nearly at the drive gates. Pulling to the side, he got out, and opened the trunk of the car.

Inside were two paintings, and a beautifully polished wooden box.

He did not attempt to study the paintings, but taking the box to the front of the car, placed it on the seat next to him. He looked at it for a long time from every angle, then, lifting it, shook it gently from side to side; nothing rattled. He held it close to his ear, tipping it up and down; and this time there was a movement, soft, flowing, as of liquid. Very quietly he got out of the car, holding the box in both hands before him. Raising it above his head he hurled it as far as he could throw. It hit the ground fifty or sixty feet away from him, smashed—and then burst into flames! On the instant fire seared the grass for a radius of at least two yards. Had he opened that box close to his face, it would have blinded him for life.

He watched the flames grimly.

145

He had suspected for some time what kind of psychopathic killer he was dealing with; now he knew for certain that Lobb would kill on sight, and that there was no easy way of fooling him.

Mannering went back to the car, driving soberly to the Manor. Here, the usual crop of gardeners were at work and everything seemed normal. He went in by the open front door and heard Cunliffe's voice.

"Nonsense, my dear, nonsense. You must stay at the house. Won't hear of anything different—won't hear of it." Cunliffe turned round as Mannering went into the room. "Ah! Mannering. Hoped you would be in to lunch; wanted to talk to you. You've heard about the disaster at my sister's place?"

"Yes, indeed," said Mannering. "A terrible thing."

"Isn't the place, so much," said Cunliffe, "but the contents. You, particularly, Mannering, will be able to appreciate the gravity of the loss, though it is very hard to calculate in material terms. Who would be able to value her miniatures? She had nearly as many as I have, Mannering. And her tapestries—dreadful loss, quite dreadful. And some of the most beautiful wood-carving—Violet, my dear, it hurts me to think of it."

"Oh, well," said Lady Markly, almost tonelessly, "I'm sure I shall get over it, Clive. It's very sad, but then I never did have the same feeling for old things that you have. And they *were* fully insured."

"Hear that?" Cunliffe asked Mannering wryly. "Barbarian isn't she? What will you have?"

Mannering looked at Lady Markly, trying to interpret the slight smile which played about her lips.

"It's hard to think so—and very brave of her to take the loss so philosophically," he said at last. "I'm told the cottage was absolutely gutted. May I have a dry sherry?"

"Of course, of course. Just like that cottage in the village," Cunliffe went on. "Almost as if there was a *purpose* in burning it down."

"I'm much more worried about the possibility of there having been a body," said Lady Markly.

"*Body!*" ejaculated Mannering. Once again he pretended astonishment.

"The police and some experts are over at the scene now; they *think* there may have been a thief in the cottage. Ah, sherry, Mr. Mannering."

They had luncheon.

Lady Markly went up to her room.

"Mannering," said Cunliffe, almost as soon as she had gone, "I'm very worried indeed. First Eliza Doze's cottage burnt to the ground, now Violet's. And then that fire that nearly started in the studio. I thought Joanna was responsible, but now I hardly know what to think. Imagine this magnificent old house going up in smoke!" He began to pace the room, looking out on to the beautiful ornamental garden as he did so. "Why *should* anyone wish to burn the place down, Mannering?"

Mannering frowned. "Are you having a special watch kept tonight?"

"Oh, yes. The police are vigilant enough, but they can't protect the place for ever. It's dreadful," muttered Cunliffe, straightening his shoulders as if bracing himself to face a hostile world. "Oh, well——" He broke off and hurried from the room.

Mannering went upstairs feeling very thoughtful. There were several things he wanted to tell the police, but he was loath to telephone them from here, equally loath to go into Salisbury again. Undecided, he passed the door next to Joanna's room—and heard a click. Instantly, he was on the alert.

He heard a whisper.

"*Mr. Mannering.*"

He glanced over his shoulder at the door.

"*Mr. Mannering.*"

Lady Markly was standing there, beckoning him urgently.

As soon as he was inside the room, she took his arm. "I don't want to upset my brother," she went on in the same conspiratorial manner, "he's worried enough already, but there are things I think you should know."

Her eyes, very clear, very intelligent, looked into his, and the pressure of her fingers on his arm was tight.

"What kind of things?" Mannering asked.

"If I tell you in confidence, will you promise not to say a word to my brother *or* to the police?" demanded Lady Markly.

CHAPTER EIGHTEEN

CONFIDENCES

It was one thing to lie to Lobb and his like; quite another to lie to a woman in his own sphere. Mannering had to weigh up the possibility of having to break a promise so as to help Joanna and to find out the truth—and at the same time he had to form a quick opinion of this woman's intelligence.

"I won't tell your brother," he said at last, "but I might have to tell the police."

"And *they* might have to tell my brother!"

"Yes."

"You're a very rare thing," said Violet Markly. "An honest man. Well, that's a chance we'll have to take. Mr. Mannering"—she drew back, looking steadily into Mannering's eyes—"I'm very worried about Joanna."

"I think we all should be worried about her," said Mannering.

"She *is* in trouble."

"Do you know what trouble?"

"No. But I know what she has been doing to try to get out of it," Violet Markly told him.

"What?" asked Mannering softly.

"Stealing pictures from her father's collection, substituting copies and selling the originals through dishonest dealers who have cheated and blackmailed her," Lady Markly said with great precision.

"And why do you think this?" Mannering demanded.

"I began to suspect it about six months ago. After I'd paid a surprise visit to the studio and seen copies of two of my brother's paintings."

"Does she know you've seen these copies?"

"No. I went to the studio one day when she was with Hester in London," Lady Markly said. There was not a moment's hesitation about her answers. "And I didn't tell her, I simply waited."

Mannering frowned. "If you'd told her, you might have helped."

"If I'd told her, I might have driven her away from me for life," retorted Lady Markly. "Now, when everything comes out and it's all over, she will turn to me. I can be very patient."

"So I see. What do you expect to happen now?" demanded Mannering.

"I really don't know," said Lady Markly. "Joanna's safe in the hospital, that's the most important thing so far as I'm concerned. I hope all this violence and burning will be over before she comes home."

"What do you think the violence is all about?" asked Mannering.

"If you really want my opinion, it is this." Lady Markly frowned in concentration, choosing her words deliberately. "I believe that Joanna has reached the end of her tether. She really can't go on any longer—it isn't in the child's nature to lie. I think she's told the men who are blackmailing her, and now that they've done their worst, they're trying to destroy any evidence they feel might incriminate them," Lady Markly went on. "That's my opinion."

"A final coup and a complete disappearance—yes,"

Mannering mused. "Do you know why they started on me?"

"No. And I don't *know* these men. But I have seen Joanna talking to the footman, Anstiss—who has disappeared, I understand. And I've seen Anstiss talking to a man who is supposed to work for the tree-felling company in the park—a big, powerful fellow. I think his name is Lobb."

"It is," Mannering said. "Lady Markly—Violet—have you *any* idea what Joanna did to put herself at these people's mercy?"

Lady Markly lifted her hands helplessly. "None at all. I just can't imagine *how* the child got tied up with anything like this. John"—she looked anxiously up at Mannering—"*must* you tell the police all this?"

"Not yet," Mannering reassured her. "But if you're right—and I rather think you are—it won't be easy to get Joanna out of this scrape unless the police have the whole story."

"No," Lady Markly said, slowly. "No, I suppose not. Poor Joanna. She is the only one who knows all the truth."

Mannering frowned. "I wonder."

"What do you mean by that?"

"I don't really know exactly what I do mean," said Mannering uneasily. "Unless——" He broke off, the flaming cottage glowing in his mind's eye. "What do you know of Eliza Doze?" he asked.

"She's a self-opinionated, stubborn, fanatically loyal and faithful old woman," answered Violet Markly, and a smile broke through the sadness in her eyes. "I was going to bring her to my cottage tomorrow to convalesce, but now she'll have to come here. She was my nurse and Joanna's nurse—nurse, indeed, to most of the family."

"Trustworthy?"

"Absolutely."

"Well, well," Mannering said. "I think I'm beginning to see part of the truth." He took Lady Markly's hands and gripped them tightly. "Do something for me."

"If I can."

"Telephone Chief Inspector Fishlock and tell him that Lobb made another attempt to kill me this afternoon."

"John!"

"Don't worry too much—I'm substantial evidence to the fact that he failed. And say I hope to look in and see him between five-thirty and six o'clock." Mannering moved towards the door as he spoke, raised a hand to her and went out.

The landing, staircase and hallway were empty. His car stood where he had left it and he opened the driving-seat door and got inside—then got out again and lifted the hood, suddenly fearful that there might be a booby trap.

Everything beneath the hood was quite normal.

He laughed at himself, got back into the car and turned the key in the ignition. Driving straight to Salisbury Infirmary, he asked for Dr. Ignatzi.

"As a matter of fact, sir, he's in the physiotherapy department," the receptionist said. "That's outside, through that doorway and——"

"Send a message telling him that I'm with Mrs. Eliza Doze, will you?" Mannering said, and started for the stairs. He knew that Eliza was now in a general ward of eight beds, and found her sitting up, earphones tight to her head, a rapt expression on her face. As Mannering went towards her, she started, frowned, waved to him to sit on a chair, and kept him waiting for fully three minutes. Then she took off the earphones.

"Those Beatles!" she rejoiced. "They're a scream."

"Eliza," Mannering said, "you're a wicked old woman."

"There aren't many of us left." She grinned as if with very great pride.

"Perhaps that's a good thing. What was your real reason for sending for me?"

She gave him a look of indescribable cunning.

"To see if you could tell good pictures from bad ones, of course."

"The truth, Eliza."

"What makes you think I haven't told you the truth?"

"Eliza," Mannering said, "Joanna Cunliffe is in a private ward here. She was nearly killed."

"But she *wasn't* killed, sir—and she's quite safe now."

"Eliza." Mannering leaned forward. "Did you send for me because you knew she was in great trouble and you thought I might be able to help?"

The bright, deep-set eyes were wary.

"Supposing I did."

"And did you arrange it with Lady Markly?"

The old woman scowled, and for a few moments he thought that she was going to refuse to answer. He leaned nearer, looking very straight into eyes both surprised and angry.

"And did your grand-daughter know?"

"That prattling little brat!" Eliza burst out. "Listening at doors, too! Why, if she was my child—yes, she knew all right. She overheard her ladyship and me talking. Her ladyship seemed to think you might be able to help; goodness knows what put such an idea into her head."

Mannering was smiling grimly.

"Now tell me the rest. Did Joanna ask if she could hide those paintings in your attic?"

"None of your business!"

"And had she hidden other paintings there?"

"I never said she hid *any*."

"But she did, didn't she?"

"No, she didn't," cried Eliza, "and I don't——"

Mannering interrupted her. "Did *you* hide the paintings there, *for* Joanna, and leave them until someone came to take them away on your days out?"

153

Eliza tossed her head. "If I can't do a little thing like that for a child I once dandled on my knee——"

"Eliza," Mannering said gravely, "Eliza—*if* you love Joanna, tell me the truth now. She's still in very great trouble."

"Lady Violet told me she'd made sure she would be brought here and looked after until——" Eliza stopped short, and caught her breath as she realized the significance of what she was saying. Her stare became a wary probe to judge whether Mannering had noticed it.

He let it pass.

It meant, of course, that Lady Markly had given Joanna the morphia, believing this to be the best way to make sure she was taken away from the Manor; there had been no attempted murder.

"The truth, Eliza, about Joanna," he insisted.

"She's been in great fear for a long time," declared Eliza, "and I've helped her any way I could. But last week she seemed more frightened than ever, and that brute Lobb came back. Whenever he was in the district she was worse, he frightened the life out of her. We knew the Colonel would never forgive us if we went to the police, but Lady Violet thought *you* might help."

The old woman paused, and after a moment took Mannering's hands, drew him towards her and went on in a quick but husky voice:

"You've got to make the child talk. You've got to. *I've* tried, her ladyship's tried, and we haven't managed to get any of the truth out of her, but *you've* got to find it out. She's the only one who knows, don't you understand? She's the only one."

Mannering thought: You're probably right, Eliza.

And then he wondered: How can I make her talk?

As he was asking himself that question there was a sound behind him, and Dr. Ignatzi appeared. One moment Mannering felt pleasure at seeing him, the next he felt a searing surge of alarm, for there was livid fear on the doctor's face.

"Joanna has been taken from her ward," he said harshly. "The ambulance driver had written authority signed by Colonel Cunliffe. I've just telephoned the Colonel, who says he knows nothing about it."

CHAPTER NINETEEN

JOANNA LOST

Mannering, Chief Inspector Fishlock, Ignatzi and several policemen and hospital staff were in the small courtyard at the side of the hospital. A short man in a white smock, with a round head and a very pale face, spoke with a north country accent.

"No, he wasn't one of our drivers, sir."

"What did he look like?" demanded Fishlock.

"He was a big man, with strong features and very thin lips."

"Lobb," Fishlock said, grimly. "You should never——"

"But he *did* have a letter from Colonel Cunliffe, sir!"

"Yes, so it seems," Mannering said. "How long ago was this?"

"I put it down in the book, sir. It was at five twenty-seven."

"Twenty minutes ago," muttered Ignatzi. "She could be dead by now."

"It isn't my fault," said the round-headed man, "it really isn't. We often have patients called for by private ambulances. It can't have gone far."

A policeman with a walkie-talkie radio broke in excitedly. "The ambulance has been seen, sir." He was listening intently, earphones at his ear. "A converted

Humber Super Snipe, yes . . . didn't get the number but it started with PRV . . . Where? . . . Well, get after it and——"

"Give me that." Fishlock grabbed the radio. "Chief Inspector Fishlock here. Concentrate all cars on that area and call for assistance from Hampshire and Dorset. Right." He switched off. "The ambulance was heading for Marlborough on the back road. There are several cuts across towards the Manor." He touched a sergeant on the shoulder. "Raid The Kettle. Send a car out to the head office of the tree-felling company. I'll alert Colonel Cunliffe."

"You surely don't think he'd take her to the Manor, do you?" demanded Ignatzi.

"Don't you think it's possible, Mr. Mannering?"

"Just possible," Mannering said. "If he's making a last coup he might use Joanna to bring pressure on her father. Coming with me, doctor?"

"I wish I could, but I must see some patients," Ignatzi said gruffly.

"I'll be with you later." Mannering was already moving to the back of the hospital where he had parked his car. The late afternoon sun shone brightly on the cathedral spire as it rose high and pure above the roofs of the city.

"I'll see you there!" called Fishlock.

Mannering swung out of the parking place, trying to remember exactly how to get to The Kettle. Stopping the car, he hailed one of Fishlock's men.

"Guide me to The Kettle, will you?"

"Right, sir." The man clambered in beside him.

As they approached the narrow gateway which led into the Close, a car, just in sight, stopped and waved them on.

"Luck's with us, sir."

"I hope to God it's with that girl." Mannering accelerated as he spoke, and two or three people who

157

were standing in the road, their cameras pointing at the cathedral, skipped out of the way.

"Shouldn't overdo speed here, sir."

Mannering grunted.

They turned left, out of another wider gateway some distance from the cathedral. Two more turns and they were pulling up outside The Kettle. The *Closed* sign was up at the door. Mannering took one look at the lock, and knew that he could force it in two minutes with his picklock, but such dexterity practiced under the eye of the law could have repercussions.

The policeman shouldered him aside.

"Excuse me, sir." Mannering stood, tactfully idle, as the man bent over the door. The lock clicked, and he turned the handle and pushed. The door opened. "It was closed from the outside, no one's in," he remarked in a tone of disappointment.

Mannering strode forward to the inner room, found it empty, then went on to the kitchen.

Dora Jenkins lay back in a rocking chair, as if she were fast asleep. Her husband, whom Mannering had seen only for those few minutes at Quinns, was on an upright chair, lolling against the sink. Mannering stepped to Dora and felt her pulse, then dropped her arm, for he could see that she was breathing. The policeman gave a long whistle as he raised Jenkins's eyelid.

"Morphia, sir."

"Get 'em to hospital," Mannering said.

"Right, sir!"

Mannering ran across the road between two cars approaching from different directions. One man glared, the other's horn shrieked in protest. Mannering took the wheel of his own car and started the engine almost in the same movement. Swinging into a clear road he settled back. It was no use taking wild chances to save a couple of minutes, he must discipline himself. Once he was beyond the city outskirts he could put on speed.

Lobb had made sure his sister and brother-in-law could not talk for a few hours, which meant that he thought he needed only a few hours for a getaway. Everything he had done in the last few days suggested a desperate determination to gain time for some vital purpose.

He had killed Anstiss.

He had tried three times to kill him, Mannering.

He had not killed his sister or Jenkins.

What special reason did he have for wanting Anstiss and himself dead? The obvious one was that he thought they knew enough to damn him—or to stop him from what he was doing.

What *was* he doing?

Dealing in faked old masters and possibly with other treasures, but what had given such urgency to the situation? Simply the threat from him, Mannering?

Mannering drew near the drive gates of the Manor and in the distance saw a car coming towards him. It was coming very fast, its blinker went on and it beat him by twenty years to the gates and swung through them; there were two uniformed policemen in it. Two men working with chain saws stopped and gaped, and a little knot of gardeners gathered in the drive. The police car drew up, and Mannering stopped just behind it. He was getting out when the men came up to him.

"I'm Mannering," he said.

"Thought I recognized you," one man said. "Mr. Fishlock told us to be guided by you."

"Get all exits covered," Mannering said. "Lobb may be in there." Hurrying towards the front door, he stopped to speak to one of the gardeners. "Has Miss Joanna been brought back?"

"Yes, sir, by the side entrance," the man told him.

That was something.

"And Lobb—the driver?"

"He carried her in, sir."

Mannering strode into the hall.

Standing at the foot of the stairs was Violet Markly. At the top was Colonel Cunliffe. Both had their backs to Mannering. Middleton, hovering in the hall, was the first to notice Mannering and turn towards him.

"What's going on?" Mannering demanded.

"Something—something dreadful, sir."

Violet Markly glanced round, and said in a very calm but distant voice:

"Lobb is in the library, with Joanna. He says that he will set fire to the child if he isn't given clear passage."

"Why did he come back here?"

"I—I simply don't know." Lady Markly gripped Mannering's hand. He felt her tension as well as saw it in her face. "I just don't know. Can't you——?"

Mannering went quickly up the stairs, to Colonel Cunliffe. Cunliffe did not seem to notice; his face was the color of white marble, his eyes like glass. When Mannering gripped his arm he felt the icy coldness through the sleeve.

"What does he want?" Mannering demanded roughly.

Cunliffe muttered: "He mustn't kill her. *He mustn't kill her!*"

"What does he *want?*"

"My—my keys," said Cunliffe.

"*Keys?*"

"Keys to—my strong-room in London. He——"

"What's in the strong-room?"

"A fortune," cried Cunliffe. "Everything—everything." He pressed a hand against his forehead. "If—if I don't give them to him and—and help him get away, he'll—he'll burn Joanna to death."

"Where are the keys?" demanded Mannering.

"I—I have them here. He—he thought they were in the library, he——"

"Who are you talking to?" Lobb called out, his voice so powerful that it boomed even through the closed door.

Cunliffe's right hand was at his pocket.

"You heard me!" Lobb roared. "Who's out there?"

Footsteps sounded very softly on the stairs, and Fishlock whispered from just behind Mannering: "We can't let him go. You know that."

"You might have to."

"Who's talking out there?" demanded Lobb. "Tell me, or I'll strike a match!"

Mannering called: "This is Mannering." He paused, to let this sink in, then added: "What do you want, Lobb?"

"I want Cunliffe's keys, and I want a clear passage back to the car. *Hear me?*"

"I can hear you."

"And if you're such pals with the police, you tell them I'll have the girl in the car with me and if they try to stop me anywhere on the road I'll start a fire with her."

"You'd only kill yourself," Mannering pointed out.

"Do what I tell you, or I'll start it *now!*" Lobb roared.

"He will," muttered Cunliffe. "He's quite capable of it. He'll kill himself rather than be caught. I'm sure of it."

"Don't be a fool, Lobb," Mannering called. "Come and give yourself up, they don't hang you these days."

"I'm not going to argue. You fix the police, *now*, or I'll kill Joanna. Colonel—I want those keys. Don't try to fool me, I'll recognize them all right. Put them in the ante-room, and then go out and lock the door."

"It's no use having the keys if you can't get away," Mannering called. "I'll talk to the police——"

"Don't try any tricks, Mannering. Once I start the fire it will be all over in a few minutes. It's up to you to make them understand that."

"I'll talk to them," Mannering promised. He motioned to Fishlock and spoke quietly to Cunliffe. "Stall as long as you can. Take the keys into the ante-room and plead with him there. Do you understand?"

Cunliffe simply looked dazed but Violet Markly, now on the landing, nodded to Mannering.

"Leave it to me," she said. "You go on."

Lobb began to bellow his orders as Mannering and Fishlock went downstairs. Fishlock said jerkily:

"We can let him out of the house. Stop him on the road. Obviously can't let him go. Man's a murderer. And insane. My God, what a situation."

"You start stalling when Cunliffe comes out," Mannering said: "Give me a quarter of an hour at least."

"What are you going to do?"

"I'm going in by the window," declared Mannering.

Fishlock stopped short. "But that's our job!"

"No time to argue," Mannering told him. "I know the wall, I was examining it last night—I can get up there. I've all the tools I need and a tear-gas pistol in a waistband." He tapped his flat stomach briskly.

"Mannering, don't you understand? He *will* start that fire!"

"If I give him time."

"He'll kill you on sight!"

Mannering said stiffly: "Get your men round the place, in sight of the window. Cause any distraction you like."

"If there's even a chance of getting that girl out——" Fishlock began.

"Not a ghost of a chance," Mannering said. "If there were, I'd be with you, but she knows far too much. He'll use her as a shield to get away, and then kill her. If she's got a chance, it's while she's in that room." They went outside and he went on: "Don't make a point of looking —but do you see that ledge which runs all round the house?"

Fishlock nodded.

"I know the one you mean."

"I can get up to it without a ladder and work my way round," Mannering said, adding with a laugh: "There are some advantages in mountaineering! Then I'll climb

162

above the window and get in from there," he continued. "If Lobb gets suspicious he might look down, but he isn't likely to look up." They were walking close to the house, out of sight of the upper windows. "The vital thing is to make sure your men are in sight but *don't* look towards me. Better clear the area of staff and locals, they'd be sure to give the game away."

"I'll fix it," Fishlock said. "And I'll have a couple of ladders handy in case you get into difficulties. Good luck, sir."

"Thanks," said Mannering.

Fishlock hurried off to begin his part of the operation, while Mannering went to the south side of the Manor to a spot where there was a recess, built as a sun-trap, with garden seats close to the wall. Here there were ledges of masonry running horizontally from the ground to the roof, and these would give him foothold. If the place had been designed for cat-burglars it could not have been more convenient.

He could climb up the inner wall of the recess without being seen.

He waited only two or three minutes, then took off his coat, secured a length of rope around his waist and put the tools he needed into his trouser pockets. Then he began to climb. Almost at once he discovered one danger —lichen had gathered on some parts of the ledges, making them very slippery. But luckily he was wearing rubber-soled shoes, which gave him a fair grip, and soon he was more than his own height above the ground.

He was just able to get a finger-hold on one ledge while standing on the other, but the climb was going to take him longer than he had thought. He needed thirty minutes, not fifteen.

How far had he to go? Two more ledges, he judged, and then he would be on the level above the library.

His fingers slipped. He leaned heavily against the wall,

163

breathing hard. But there was no time to relax, he must hurry—and haste in these conditions could send him crashing to the ground.

He began to sweat.

The higher ledges were more slippery. He put his fingers on the one he wanted to reach but could not get a hold. Pressed against the wall, he edged along, groping every few inches, until he found a purchase. Very gradually he hauled himself up, got a knee on the ledge and finally stood on it.

He looked round.

The police cordon seemed a long way off. Two or three men were staring at the windows but none were looking at him. Now he was on the right level he could move much more quickly, but it must be twenty minutes at least since he had started out, and there was no telling what Lobb had done.

A last he neared the library window, noting that it was open almost a foot at the top. He heard nothing, and was terribly afraid that Lobb might have killed Joanna and planned to escape some other way.

Then he heard Lobb roar:

"If I haven't got those keys in two minutes, I'll set her alight."

CHAPTER TWENTY

REASON FOR FEAR

Directly above the window there was a border of jutting stonework, on which Mannering decided to loop the free end of the rope. He secured it, tugged, then leaned his weight against it. Taking the gas pistol out of his pocket, he put it inside his shirt so that it couldn't fall, lowered himself until he lay along the ledge at full length, then gradually turned until his head and shoulders hung over the ledge. This was the time of greatest testing, for now he had no foothold—only his hands and arms for support, and the rope round his waist. Edging along until he was still above the window but at one side of it, he lowered himself still further, until he could see into the room.

First, he saw Joanna, stretched on Cunliffe's desk, apparently unconscious.

Then he saw two of the plastic fire-bombs, one on her breast, one at her feet. And on a corner of the desk was a box of matches. Lobb was standing with his back to the window, one hand raised and clenched, head back as he shouted:

"I mean what I say. Understand? I'll set her alight!"

Mannering slipped the pistol from his shirt. Keeping it steady as he hung down wasn't easy, but the window was open so wide that he could fire without warning. He saw

Lobb shake his fist at the door and then, incensed, swing round.

Mannering fired.

The tear-gas pellet caught Lobb on the forehead, and he started back in alarm. In the instant before the gas got into his eyes he saw Mannering, but there was no cognition. He made a dive towards the matches and Mannering fired again, but before the second pellet struck, Lobb was beginning to sway on his feet, clawing at his face.

Mannering pushed the window down further, climbed inside, undid the rope and called: "Coming!" He held his breath as he raced across to the door, turned the key and pushed back the bolts. The tear-gas began to blind his eyes as he staggered on to the landing, but men wearing improvised masks ran past him, to get Lobb and the girl.

"Mannering, I shall never be able to thank you enough —never." Cunliffe held Mannering's hand tightly, as in a vice. "It was the most courageous thing I have ever heard of—quite the most courageous. My darling Joanna—you saved my darling Joanna."

Standing beside him was Lady Markly; Fishlock and another policeman stood near. Lobb was on his way to the Salisbury police station under strong guard, Joanna was already back at the hospital and Ignatzi had just telephoned to say that her condition was improving. Over an hour had passed since the rescue, and the excitement outside had not yet died away.

"Would it be wise to check your safe?" Fishlock asked Cunliffe.

"I don't think it's necessary," Cunliffe told him. "And now, unless you have essential business here, Chief Inspector, I would appreicate it if you will leave us."

Fishlock signaled to his men and Mannering went with them to the front door. Fishlock squared his shoulders and quite unexpectedly held out his hand. "It's been a great pleasure to know you, Mr. Mannering."

Mannering smiled. "I wish all policemen were like you," he said warmly.

The police car moved off, watched by a group of estate workers and tenants from the village, and Mannering rejoined Cunliffe and his sister. Almost at once, Betsy appeared.

"Excuse me, sir, there's a telephone call for Mr. Mannering."

"Thank you, where——?"

"Where's Middleton?" demanded the Colonel, sharply.

"He's not very well, sir."

"Ah. Excitement too much for him, I suppose. Where's the call?"

"In the morning-room, sir. It's a Mr. Larraby."

Mannering went into the morning-room, and picked up the telephone. He felt overwhelmingly tired, but knew he had to steel himself to make one more effort.

"Hallo, Josh," he said. "It's all right to say whatever you want to say."

"That blackmail note, sir. It was definitely written by Lobb; the handwriting people have compared it with a letter on the police files, and there's no doubt about it. As for those two pictures which had been over-painted, they were superimposed on recent copies—excellent copies, but copies nevertheless. One was a Vermeer, the other a Franz Hals. Is that what you expected, sir?"

"Yes," Mannering said. "Just what I expected." He paused. "Josh—tell young Willis to bring Hester down here at once—she'll be needed." He replaced the receiver and went back into the hall, where Cunliffe was standing before one of the ancestral portraits, while his sister walked aimlessly to and fro. There was an atmosphere of anti-climax; neither Cunliffe nor Lady Markly seemed to know exactly what to do. Mannering waited long enough to be sure they knew he was back, then announced clearly:

"That was a most interesting case."

Cunliffe spun round.

"Was that from the police? Has Lobb talked?"

"No," Mannering said. "Joanna has."

"Joanna?" Lady Markly came forward very quickly. "But she is still unconscious, she can't have talked!"

"That was her great trouble, wasn't it," Mannering said grimly. "She could never bring herself to talk."

"Mannering, be good enough to make your meaning clear," Cunliffe said coldly.

"I shall do precisely that," Mannering said. "What do you think is the cause of Joanna's strange behavior?"

"She——" Cunliffe began, then broke off.

"Why did she paint her little trifles over old masters?" demanded Mannering.

Cunliffe caught his breath.

"You *know* that. Oh, dear God." He became old and defeated in one moment, shoulders sagging, hands limp by his side. "This is—dreadful. I've realized for some time what she has been doing. Mannering, I—I should have told the police. I realize that. But how can one betray one's own flesh and blood? How *can* one?" He began to wring his hands. "She had copies painted and replaced the real ones with the copies; then—then she had the real ones sold. She painted over them so that—so that she could get them out of the house without being discovered. She must have got into the wrong hands, Mannering. It's not her fault, I can't bring myself to blame her. The man Lobb exerted great pressure, intolerable pressure. Poor child, she——"

"You are a nauseating hypocrite," Mannering said clearly.

Cunliffe gasped.

"I will repeat that," said Mannering. "You are a nauseating hypocrite, Cunliffe."

"You—you are insulting, sir!"

"Yes," Mannering said. "I mean to be."

"You yourself said that my daughter painted over old masters——"

"She painted over *faked* old masters," said Mannering, "in a desperate, last-minute attempt to save you, her father, from being unmasked as a swindler. As soon as she realized I was a picture-expert she was afraid I'd discover the fakes and would guess what was going on—*that* was why she painted over them."

"John, what are you saying?" demanded Lady Markly tensely.

Mannering turned towards her. "I am saying that your brother hired this fellow Lobb to paint copies of certain paintings in his collection. These copies he sold as genuine, and had the originals stored in his London vault."

Cunliffe was standing very still.

"Clive," said his sister in a strained voice. "Clive you——!" She broke off. Mannering's expression as he looked at Cunliffe was one of utter disgust.

"Joanna found out and tried to stop you, but you would not stop," he said. "As soon as Lobb discovered how concerned she was, and how afraid that you might be discovered, he began to blackmail her—while you stood by and allowed him to do so."

Cunliffe said thinly: "I had no choice."

"You mean you refused to consider one."

"We were both in that man's hands. When I first employed him I thought I could trust him. Then, too late, I found that I couldn't."

"So that was it," breathed Lady Markly.

"That was it," said Mannering flatly. "Joanna did everything she could to protect her father, and paid all she had to Lobb to try to save him. But there came a time when she could go on no longer. Then, at Lobb's instigation, she *did* steal old masters—hiding them in Eliza Doze's attic. Eliza knew they were there but didn't know their value nor what they were. She *did* see Joanna being

169

driven to despair, and she sent for me." He did not betray his knowledge of Lady Markly's share in that.

"So it *was* Joanna who took the paintings from the north gallery," muttered Cunliffe. "Oh well,"—he shrugged his shoulders—"it doesn't matter now." He looked from Mannering to Lady Markly, then back to Mannering. "I had no choice," he repeated hoarsely, "no choice at all."

"You knew Joanna was near breaking-point, but you did nothing to help her," said Mannering.

"I had no choice," Cunliffe repeated yet again, as if these were words graven on his mind. "I had to preserve the family honor. And I had to preserve the family position. With taxation as savage as it is, some effort must be made to live as one was ordained to live. I could either sell my treasures, or—make copies and sell to the fools who thought they were real. I did my duty as I conceived it."

"You condemned your daughter to despair," said Mannering quietly. "You allowed Lobb the sadistic touch of shearing her hair, and threatening her with even worse violence. To lull any suspicions I might have, you said that she was either mad or bad—or both. And only a few moments ago you tried to shield yourself at her expense. Where are the original paintings now? Still in the vault in London?"

"They are. And they are *mine*. I have preserved one of the greatest private collections of works of art. I have maintained Nether Manor in its rightful way. I have continued to employ servants who were the children of servants for many generations. And my daughter betrayed me."

His sister was looking at him in mingled horror and disgust.

Mannering stepped forward. "She never betrayed you. You betrayed yourself."

170

Cunliffe gasped. "You mean she didn't—she didn't tell you——?" His voice tailed away.

"No," said Mannering. "She didn't tell me. She didn't tell anyone."

"Then—then what you have just said was all—*was all bluff?*"

Mannering nodded. "Partly. And you confirmed my suspicions. But don't think that Lobb wouldn't have given you away. Do you seriously think he will take the blame for all this without naming you?"

Cunliffe didn't answer.

"Because he won't," Mannering went on. "The moment he realizes that he hasn't a chance, that will be the moment he'll start talking about your share in the crimes."

Cunliffe gave an almost imperceptible nod, then turned and walked away. His footsteps echoed on the porch, sounded on the gravel of the drive, then petered into silence.

Violet Markly turned towards Mannering. "You know what he will do, don't you?"

"I know what I expect him to do," Mannering said. "He could never bring himself to face trial."

"You understand so much, don't you?" said Lady Markly slowly.

"So much was obvious," Mannering murmured. "I began to suspect your brother might be involved just after I put out a fire in the studio beneath the north gallery. He came down while I was in the studio, but I stepped behind an easel and I didn't think he saw me—but a little later he pretended to confide in me; told me that there had always been throwbacks to evil strains and insanity in the Cunliffe family, and blamed Joanna for the fire. I knew then that he must have known I was there."

"But who started the fire?" asked Lady Markly.

"Lobb or Anstiss, I imagine, in an attempt to burn any incriminating evidence. *They* didn't care if the Manor burnt to the ground, and they knew by then that I was on to them. But it'll all come out at the trial. Violet"—Mannering looked directly at Lady Markly—"tell me one thing."

"If I can."

"Did *you* drug Joanna after her collapse?"

"I couldn't see her suffer any more," Lady Markly said simply. "I thought that was the best way to help her. I wanted to get her out of this house and away from any further danger, so I gave her a slight overdose of sleeping tablets, crushed in milk—I *think* they contained morphia, but I can't show them to you because the bottle's completely disappeared. I suppose Clive took them."

"It was Lobb who took them," said Mannering. "He gave them to his sister and her husband—Mr. and Mrs. Jenkins of The Kettle—to keep them quiet during his intended getaway. Well, that's solved the mystery of how he came by them. Violet, let me ask you something——"

"No, let *me* ask *you* something," said Violet Markly. "Tell me—were *you* in my cottage last night?"

Mannering smiled faintly. "Yes—I'm afraid I'd been wondering if you were involved. Please forgive me. But if I hadn't found those pictures in your attic——"

Lady Markly looked startled. "What pictures?"

"Joanna's pictures—the pictures which gave me the final answers to this whole mystery. I first came across them in the studio, and noticed that he'd painted over what appeared, on first inspection, to be something pretty valuable. They were, of course, two of Lobb's faked old masters, which Joanna was afraid I'd recognize and had, in a desperate attempt to protect her father, painted over. While I was taking them to Salisbury, someone—I suspect Lobb—ran me down in a lorry, and the pictures disappeared. Lobb, if it was Lobb, must have given them to your brother. He, realizing I must be sus-